PRAISE FOR BRUCE CATTON
AND *GETTYSBURG:THE FINAL FURY*

"No one ever wrote American history with more easy grace, beauty and emotional power, or greater understanding of its meaning, than Bruce Catton. There is a near-magic power of imagination in Catton's work that seemed to project him physically into the battlefields, along the dusty roads and to the campfires of another age."

—Oliver Jensen,
former editor of *American Heritage*

"[Catton combines] a scholar's appreciation of the Grand Design with a newsman's keenness for meaningful vignette.... Catton created an 'enlisted man's-eye view' of the war that treated humanely the errors on both sides."   —*Newsweek*

"All [of Catton's Civil War books] are remarkably good books, distinguished by a vivid, fast-moving style."

—*The New York Times Book Review*

"One of the most skillful old pros that the craft [of historical narrative] h   ˙*Books*

D1530273

ALSO BY BRUCE CATTON

The War Lords of Washington

Mr. Lincoln's Army

Glory Road

This Hallowed Ground

A Stillness at Appomattox

U. S. Grant and the American Military Tradition

Banners at Shenandoah:
A Story of Sheridan's Fighting Cavalry

This Hallowed Ground

America Goes to War

The American Heritage Picture History of the Civil War

The American Heritage Short History of the Civil War

Grant Moves South

The Coming Fury

Terrible Swift Sword

Two Roads to Sumter

Four Days: The Historical Record of the
Death of President Kennedy

Never Call Retreat

Grant Takes Command

Waiting for the Morning Train

Michigan: A Bicentennial History

The Bold and Magnificent Dream:
America's Founding Years, 1492–1815

GETTYSBURG
THE FINAL FURY

"Military history . . . at its best." —*Chicago Tribune*

BRUCE CATTON

Pulitzer Prize-winning Author of

A STILLNESS AT APPOMATTOX

BRUCE CATTON

GETTYSBURG: THE FINAL FURY

Bruce Catton was born in Petoskey, Michigan, in 1899. A United States journalist and writer, Catton was one of America's most popular Civil War historians. He worked as a newspaperman in Boston, Cleveland, and Washington, and also held a position at the U.S. Department of Commerce in 1948. Catton's bestselling book, *A Stillness at Appomattox*, earned him a Pulitzer Prize and National Book Award in 1954. Before his death in 1978, Catton wrote a total of ten books detailing the Civil War, including his last, *Grant Takes Command*.

BRUCE CATTON

Gettysburg

THE FINAL FURY

VINTAGE CIVIL WAR LIBRARY
Vintage Books
A Division of Random House, Inc.
New York

FIRST VINTAGE CIVIL WAR LIBRARY EDITION, JUNE 2013

Copyright © 1974 by Bruce Catton

All photographs, drawings, and paintings reproduced in this book are from the collections of the Library of Congress, except the two on pages 11 and 98, which are reproduced by courtesy of The Bettmann Archive, Inc. The maps are by Rafael Palacios.

The Library of Congress has cataloged the Doubleday edition as follows:
Catton, Bruce.
Gettysburg: the final fury / Bruce Catton.
p. cm.
Originally published: 1974.
Includes index.
1. Gettysburg, Battle of, 1863.
I. Title.
E475.53.C32   1990   89-23554
973.7'349—dc20

Vintage ISBN: 978-0-345-80605-5

Printed In The United States Of America
10 9 8 7 6 5 4 3 2 1

CONTENTS

———•◦•———

One
The Road to Gettysburg 3

Two
First Day: Collision 17

Three
Second Day: Fighting by Compulsion 35

Four
Third Day: Climax 69

Five
Long Remember 97

Index 111

ILLUSTRATIONS

MAPS

Gettysburg

THE FINAL FURY

One

THE ROAD TO GETTYSBURG

———•◦•———

*I*t took a strange combination of forces to bring about the terrible battle of Gettysburg. No one of these, taken by itself, was strong enough to cause such a cataclysm. Only when they were arranged together in proper sequence did these forces become deadly. The elements that make up gunpowder are harmless enough, separately; in combination they become explosive, needing only a spark or a sudden jar to set them off. The battle of Gettysburg was like that.

It was compounded partly of geography, which is to say that the armies fought at Gettysburg because the roads led them there. Sheer chance played its part in this; if various circumstances had been just a little different the unremarkable Pennsylvania market town would have remained at peace and the armies would have gone elsewhere. Military logic was responsible, in part, and so was plain human miscalculation, because it is not always easy to interpret the date that logic brings you.

Finally, the battle was fated, in that it grew out of

what the war for two years had been. It was a battle that had to be fought, and the forces that produced it were so stupendous that the battle became the great hinge of the war, the turning point where it began to swing in a different direction. But even though destiny was at work, it is still worth while to see why this great fight took place at Gettysburg instead of in some other town, on the first three days of July 1863 instead of at some other time.

Gettysburg came just two months after the most dazzling of all Confederate victories, the battle of Chancellorsville, where the Army of Northern Virginia under Robert E. Lee, who was brilliantly aided by Stonewall Jackson, defeated the Federal Army of the Potomac under Major General Joe Hooker. The Federals outnumbered the Confederates here, two to one, but Lee and Jackson between them were more than a dozen Joe Hookers could have handled, and the Federal offensive which had been supposed to capture Richmond ended in an ignominious retreat. Yet if this Confederate triumph was a work of high military art, it was actually worth less than it seemed to be worth. For one thing, Jackson was killed, and Lee's army was never again the instantly responsive precision instrument it had been. In the second place, Lee was still badly outnumbered, and the Federal army had great recuperative power; left to itself it would inevitably renew the offensive and the whole job would have to be done over again. Chancellorsville had settled nothing; it had simply set the stage for a further struggle.

In addition, if things had been going well for the Confederacy in Virginia, they had been going very badly in the Mississippi Valley. While Lee was defeating Hooker,

Major General U. S. Grant was forcing his way into the open country behind the great Confederate fortress of Vicksburg, and by the end of the third week in May he had the Confederate Lieutenant General John Pemberton and his army firmly locked up in Vicksburg, isolated and under siege. Unless somebody came to Pemberton's rescue and forced Grant to raise the siege, Vicksburg was bound to fall, and when it fell the Federals would control the entire Mississippi River. If that happened the Confederacy would be well on its way toward final defeat.

So when the Confederate authorities took stock, late in May of 1863, they could see dire emergency taking shape in the West, and that fact was bound to affect any plans that might be made for the use of Lee's army. The Secretary of War proposed that Lee detach a division of infantry and send it off to Pemberton's rescue. The division suggested for this move was one commanded by young Major General George Pickett, attached to the I Corps commanded by Lieutenant General James Longstreet. Longstreet was a solid, dependable fighting man, Lee's most trusted lieutenant now that Jackson was gone, and Longstreet considered Pickett's his best division. Lee strongly objected to this proposal, and he warned the Secretary of War that if this was the only way to save Vicksburg, the government would have to make up its mind whether it wanted to lose Mississippi or Virginia; and the fact that the Confederacy could not under any circumstances afford to lose either state simply added to the load carried by President Jefferson Davis, who would have to make the decision. Lee believed that Hooker was being reinforced and would soon resume the offensive;

his own responsibility was the defense of Virginia and the Confederate capital, and he naturally did not think he ought to be weakened.

As a matter of fact, some of President Davis's advisers thought that Vicksburg ought to be saved even if that meant taking long chances in front of Richmond. The distinguished General P. G. T. Beauregard, now commanding in South Carolina, urged that Lee be sent to Tennessee, taking Longstreet's corps with him, to take command of the Confederate army near Chattanooga commanded by General Braxton Bragg. Using Bragg's army thus augmented, Beauregard believed, Lee could stage an offensive in Tennessee that would compel the Federal government to recall Grant from Mississippi. As for Virginia—the Army of the Potomac was notoriously slow to act, and the depleted Army of Northern Virginia could probably hold it off until Lee and Longstreet's corps returned. Longstreet advanced a similar plan, except that his plan did not involve sending Lee himself to Tennessee.

In the end none of these proposals was adopted. The Confederates in the West would have to get along as best they could, and Lee—well, Lee had a daring plan of his own. He would invade Pennsylvania.

It was a bold move, bound to bring the war to a climax, and yet the reasons for it are somewhat obscure.

Then and afterward it was argued that Lee's invasion would relieve the desperate situation in Mississippi by forcing President Lincoln to withdraw support from General Grant. This argument simply does not stand up. The siege of Vicksburg began on May 19. Lee could not put his army in motion before June, and it would be the end of June before he could hope to cross the Potomac. This was giving General Grant altogether too much time; and if Lincoln wanted reinforcements to meet Lee's thrust, he would not have to reach all the way to Mississippi to get them.

It was also held that the invasion would support a Southern peace offensive. There was much war-weariness in the North, and the presence of a Confederate army in Pennsylvania would add to it—perhaps to the point where Lincoln would be forced to concede Southern independence. (The invasion might also enable the Confederacy to grasp that elusive will-o'-the-wisp British recognition.) But this would work only if Lee won an overwhelming victory in Pennsylvania. Anything short of that would only stimulate Northern energies. After all, Lee had invaded the northland in September of 1862 and had won neither a negotiated peace nor recognition by London. Instead he had been thrown back at Antietam (Sharpsburg) and Lincoln issued the Emancipation Proclamation as a direct result.

Actually, Lee's reasons for marching north seem to have been fairly simple. Sooner or later the Army of the Potomac would resume its drive on Richmond; to move north would disrupt the enemy's war plans and throw Hooker off balance; it might very well delay the renewed Yankee invasion until the following year. The Confederacy was hard pressed, and that would be a gain worth making.

In addition, the move would at least give Virginia temporary relief from a strain that had become almost intolerable. The constant struggling of the rival armies had laid

much of the state waste; if the war could be moved north
for a time that would be a distinct advantage, and Lee's
army could draw its supplies of meat and grain from the
lush farmlands of Pennsylvania. Let the North support
the war for a while; Virginia needed a chance to catch its
breath.

In plain English, then, the invasion was a matter of
limited objectives, which might be summed up in the
remark that since Lee's army was going to have to fight
somewhere this summer, it might better fight north of the
Mason and Dixon line than south of it.

The only trouble with this was that because Lee and
his army were what they were, an invasion with limited
objectives was not possible. If this army went north of the
Potomac, its venture was going to be an all-or-nothing
thrust simply because both friend and foe were bound to
look at it that way. Lee and the Army of Northern Virginia had won too many battles; they had begun to seem
invincible, both to their enemies and also to themselves.
When they went north they carried the undeveloped climax of the war with them. Win or lose, this march was
going to take them to the high-water mark.

The one strategist who realized this most clearly was
that untaught, awkward, non-military man Abraham
Lincoln.

Lincoln had had no military education before he
entered the White House, but he was a man who could
learn fast, and by the summer of 1863 he could understand a military equation as well as any man in America.
In the late spring of 1863, when something like panic
went across the North at the news that Lee was invading

Pennsylvania, Lincoln saw in the move a bright opportunity for the Federals. Coming north, Lee was exposing his army to destruction. The Federals always had the advantage in numbers; now they would have the advantage in position as well, and if they maneuvered skillfully they could cut this invading army off, hem it in, and destroy it utterly. . . . That, at any rate, is the way Lincoln saw it, and his hopes rose. Grant obviously was going to take Vicksburg. If at the same time the great Army of Northern Virginia could be taken off the board, the war would be about over.

Lee's army at the end of May lay south of the Rappahannock River, in and near Fredericksburg, with Hooker's army just north of the river keeping watch. Contrary to Lee's expectation, Hooker was not being reinforced; actually, he was losing strength because the time of a number of his volunteer regiments was expiring and thousands of good soldiers were being paid off and sent home. He still had an advantage in numbers, but his army and Lee's were more nearly on a parity in strength than they had ever been before or would be again. Lee had probably 75,000 men of all arms; Hooker may have had between 85,000 and 90,000, and Hooker's men were much better equipped and fed. As a counterweight to this, Lee's men had the habit of victory, and Hooker's had never been able to acquire that habit. All in all, the armies were fairly close to equal.

Lee's march began on June 3, when Longstreet's I Corps faded back from the Rappahannock crossings and marched northwest toward Culpeper Courthouse, to be followed a day or so later by the II Corps led by Lieutenant General Richard Ewell. Ewell was a bald, peppery

little man with a wooden leg—he had been maimed during the preliminaries to the second battle of Bull Run—
and when the army was on the march he rode in a buggy.
In battle he mounted his horse, game leg and all, and had
himself strapped to the saddle.

For rear guard at Fredericksburg, Lee left his III
Infantry Corps under Lieutenant General A. P. Hill, one
of the Confederacy's fabulous fighting men. It was not
long before Hooker saw what was happening and proposed to attack Hill in force, driving him off and moving
directly on Richmond. President Lincoln overruled him,
pointing out that Lee's army rather than the Confederate capital was Hooker's proper objective now. Hooker
began to move northwest on a course roughly parallel
with Lee's, keeping the Army of the Potomac always
between Lee and Washington.

Lee's plan was simple. He would move beyond the
Blue Ridge, cross the Potomac, and then march toward
the east, threatening Philadelphia and Baltimore, cutting
Washington's communications with the rest of the country, and putting on pressure that would force Hooker to
attack him; in effect, he would blend offensive strategy
with defensive tactics, compelling his opponent (as he
had so often done before) to fight his kind of fight. At
Chancellorsville Hooker had shown himself to be erratic
when the heat was on. When the armies met in Pennsylvania the heat would be greater than anything Hooker
had experienced before. Limited objectives or no, the
possibilities for Lee were dazzling.

On the surface, everything went smoothly. Lee handled the northward march most competently, and Hooker

never had a good chance to attack him en route. Longstreet
held his corps in and east of the Blue Ridge, Ewell smashed
a Federal outpost at Winchester and then moved boldly
north, across Maryland and into Pennsylvania; Hill followed with his corps, and when he crossed the Potomac,

This wartime lithograph, "Lee and His Generals," does show
a great many Confederate generals, although many of them
were not especially associated with Lee (except that they all
fought on the same side). Lee of course is in the center. The
more prominent other generals include P. G. T. Beauregard,
mounted, at left, with Braxton Bragg over his right shoulder;
Joseph E. Johnston, raising his hat, with heavily bearded Jeb
Stuart on his right. Mounted, on Lee's left, is James Longstreet, followed (to the right, in background) by Bedford
Forrest, John B. Hood, and A. P. Hill. Mounted in the right
foreground, is Stonewall Jackson; mounted, by Jackson's
right elbow, is Richard Ewell. (The Bettmann Archive, Inc.)

Longstreet slipped beyond the mountain wall and followed him. By the final days of June, Lee had all of his infantry and artillery above the Potomac. Ewell had gone far to the eastward and was threatening Harrisburg and York. Hill was ready to move after him, and Longstreet had his men posted at Chambersburg, awaiting developments.

By the night of June 28 Lee learned two things—that the Army of the Potomac was north of the Potomac River, instead of lying inert to the south of it as he had supposed, and that Meade had replaced Hooker as its commander. He at once ordered his army to assemble at the handiest place, which turned out to be Gettysburg. Meade, meanwhile, ordered his own army to concentrate along a little stream called Pipe Creek, which offered a good defense position covering both Washington and Baltimore, while his cavalry under Buford rode north to get a line on Lee's position. Stuart's Confederate cavalry, meanwhile, was trying desperately to regain its proper position on Lee's immediate right flank.

There was a slight question about Lee's cavalry. It was led by Major General J. E. B. ("Jeb") Stuart—flamboyant, picturesque, a headline-hunter, but an uncommonly able cavalry leader for all that: a man on whom Lee relied implicitly. Stuart had a double assignment—to screen Lee's army and to keep Lee informed all the time where Hooker's army was. When the last of Lee's infantry crossed the Potomac, Stuart was supposed to follow it and then move eastward along Lee's right flank, covering the march and making certain that Lee knew just where all the elements of the Federal army might be.

Preparing to leave Virginia, Stuart got Lee's permission to put a little extra frill on his march. The Federal army lay in camp in Virginia a few miles east of the Blue Ridge, and Stuart believed he could best get into Pennsylvania by marching entirely around this Federal army and crossing the Potomac far downstream from the crossings Lee's infantry had used. Lee approved, stipulating only that whatever he did, Stuart must get promptly to his assigned position on the invading army's right flank. On this march deep into enemy territory Lee simply had to have Stuart near him.

Stuart moved on June 25 and immediately ran into trouble. Hooker had moved up to the Potomac, and his huge army occupied all of the river crossings Stuart had planned to use. Stuart was crowded far off into eastern Virginia, Hooker got his entire army north of the river unobserved, and instead of rejoining Lee's army within thirty-six hours Stuart did not regain contact for a solid week. During that time—in some ways the most important week in his whole military career—Lee was in effect a blind man. He did not know where his enemies were.

To make matters worse, Stuart's reputation for complete reliability led Lee to make a false assumption. When days passed with no word from Stuart, Lee naturally assumed that the Army of the Potomac was inactive, remaining in its camps in Virginia; if it were on the move, Stuart would surely send word, as he had always done in the past. (Lee of course had no idea that Stuart had been blocked out of the play altogether.) If Hooker remained inactive south of the Potomac, the invading Confederates, far north of the river, could do things they would not have ventured to do if their foes were in close pursuit. So by June 28 Lee had his army spread out over a forty-five-mile crescent, Lee himself with Longstreet's corps at Chambersburg, Ewell in York and on the river bank opposite Harrisburg, Hill moving east eight or ten miles from Chambersburg. The army was dangerously dispersed, but with the Army of the Potomac south of the river this was safe enough.

Then, that evening, Lee learned that Hooker's entire army was massed in the vicinity of Frederick, Maryland. It was closer to the separate pieces of Lee's army than those pieces were to each other. Lee would be destroyed if he did not concentrate at once.

So Confederate couriers galloped off along the Pennsylvania roads that night, calling the scattered legions together. The army would assemble at Gettysburg—at Gettysburg, and not elsewhere, simply because it was central and the roads led there. The first of the accidents that would make Gettysburg a battleground had taken place. Lee's soldiers hurried as if drawn there by a magnet.

And so, for that matter, did the leading divisions of

the Army of the Potomac. They were no more interested in Gettysburg than Lee's men were. They were just groping for the enemy and this town seemed the handiest place to go groping. And as June came to an end, fate was driving thousands of soldiers toward the point of deadly collision.

Two

FIRST DAY: COLLISION

The Federal soldiers who moved toward Gettysburg were Hooker's army no longer. As they trudged along through the choking dust and the thick summer heat they were under the command of Major General George Gordon Meade, chosen by the government at Washington to replace Hooker at the moment when the greatest battle of the war was obviously just about to take place.

Hooker had been a dashing, competent soldier as leader of a division and, later, of an army corps, but the top command had somehow been too much for him. Under pressure he had simply folded up; he had fumbled his way to defeat at Chancellorsville because the responsibility of high command had paralyzed his professional faculties, and the failure had been so clearly a failure of his own nerve that he had lost the confidence of President Lincoln, not to mention that of Secretary of War Edwin M. Stanton and General in Chief Henry W. Halleck.

They had made up their minds to relieve him, but

finding a qualified successor was difficult and it was not
until the Confederate campaign of invasion was clearly
approaching its climax that the change was finally made.
They selected General Meade, who had been in command
of the V Army Corps, largely because he was known as a
reliable professional soldier who did not scare easily.

Outside of the V Corps, the soldiers had hardly so
much as heard of him, and he definitely was not the inspi-
rational leader who arouses the enthusiasm of the rank
and file. To use a modern expression, he utterly lacked
charisma. He was crusty, not to say crabbed, with a quick
temper and a sharp tongue, and he once remarked without rancor that he had heard soldiers refer to him as a
"damned goggle-eyed snapping turtle." But if his inspi-
rational qualities were nil and his strategic abilities were
unknown, there definitely was nothing wrong with his
nerves. He was not afraid of the weight of top command
and he was not in the least afraid of Robert E. Lee, and it
soon developed that when they chose Meade the authorities acted very wisely indeed.

Meade had to defend Washington, along with Philadelphia, Baltimore, and the rest of the northland, and
the only way to do this was to bring Lee to battle and
defeat him. Somewhat strung out, Lee's army was moving eastward, and Meade did not know exactly where it
was or what Lee had in mind. Sensibly enough, Meade
concluded that if he found a substantial piece of this
army and prodded it vigorously, the separate parts would
come together quickly enough. Then Lee would have to
give battle because of the conditions under which he was
operating.

Lee maintained contact with his base in Virginia, but to all intents and purposes he had abandoned his supply line and was living on the country. This Pennsylvania farm country was rich and Lee's army had had no trouble collecting food and forage—it was in fact living rather high just now—but there was one catch to all this. To live thus, the invading army had to keep moving, because if it stayed in one place very long it would consume all the supplies its immediate neighborhood produced. So far the army had kept on the march and had had no problems, but if Meade could compel it to concentrate it could not wait for him to make the attack. It would have to take the offensive or retreat; with luck, Meade would be able to make Lee attack him on ground of Meade's own choosing.

To find a suitable fragment of Lee's army, Meade sent Major General John Buford's division of cavalry north to cut across what appeared to be Lee's line of march. To molest the troops that Buford was likely to find, Meade chose Major General John Reynolds and gave him command of about one third of the army—Reynolds' own I Corps, Major General Oliver Otis Howard's XI Corps, and the III Corps under Major General Dan Sickles. On the last day of June Buford got into Gettysburg and discovered that a large body of Confederate infantry lay a few miles to the west, astride the Chambersburg road. Buford strung dismounted troopers out in a battle line on one of the low ridges a mile or so west of Gettysburg, ordered patrols off to the north to check on reports that additional Confederates were coming down from Carlisle, and sent word of all this to Reynolds, who was a

When Gettysburg is studied as a problem in strategy and tactics, attention is usually focused on General Robert E. Lee. This does some injustice to the Union commander, Major General George Gordon Meade; for if Lee lost the battle, Meade was the man who won it, and the Union cause owed a great deal to the cool competence with which he handled his army. For the first time the Army of the Potomac was under a man who refused to get nervous or uncertain when he confronted Lee on the battlefield. Meade was not a man who scared easily. . . . He is shown here in a picture made some time before Gettysburg; he wears a major general's shoulder straps but they have been tacked on to a brigadier general's coat.

short distance south of Gettysburg. Reynolds ordered his men to march for Gettysburg, and on the morning of July 1 he spurred on ahead of them to meet Buford, to get all the news Buford had, and to see for himself how the situation was developing.

It was developing fast, and fighting had already begun. Buford's troopers were firing at an advancing line of Confederate infantry, artillery had gone into action on both sides, and while Buford's men were holding the Confederates in check they obviously could not do so much longer; in a situation like this, cavalry could not hope to do much more than delay advancing infantry and force it to send out a formal line of battle. Reynolds conferred with Buford on the grounds of a Lutheran seminary near the Chambersburg road, concluded that this was a good place for a fight, and sent couriers off to bring in the leading elements of the on-coming I Corps.

The first Federal troops to come up were good ones—Brigadier General James Wadsworth's division, which included the famous Iron Brigade: western troops, known as one of the stoutest fighting units in the army. Reynolds put the westerners south of the Chambersburg road, sent Wadsworth's other brigade into action north of the road, had Buford withdraw his cavalry, and made it clear that if the Confederates wanted to occupy that ridge they would have to fight for it.

It speedily became clear that this was just what the Southerners proposed to do. They belonged to A. P. Hill's III Corps, and Hill was one of the most pugnacious soldiers in either army—tense, impetuous, a man who liked to force the fighting regardless of consequences, coming

Because rifled muskets gave infantry greatly increased fire power, the day of massed cavalry attacks on foot soldiers in the style of the Napoleonic wars had passed by the 1860s. Dismounted cavalrymen, however, could stand off an infantry attack long enough to compel the infantry commander to deploy his men in battle order, thereby displaying his strength and his intentions, and so it was on the morning of the first day's fighting at Gettysburg. On the ridges west of town, Union cavalry commander Brigadier General John Buford put his cavalry in action against Confederate infantry of Lieutenant General A. P. Hill's III Corps, delaying the Confederate advance just long enough to permit Union infantry to reach the scene. When cavalrymen fought on foot, one man in every four was detailed to hold the horses a short distance behind the fighting line; the other three used their carbines dismounted, acting precisely like infantry.

in now in the style of a heads-down slugger always willing to take a blow in order to land one. Hill had no especial reason to get into Gettysburg, but he did not need one; there were armed Yankees in front of him offering to fight, and he was going to accept their offer without delay and that was that. In place of the routine sparring that had been going on when Reynolds rode up to get Buford's situation report, an uncommonly savage battle was rapidly developing.

On July 1 Hill's III Corps struck Meade's advanced infantry, the I Corps under Reynolds, just west of Gettysburg. Howard's XI Corps came up to help the Federals just as Ewell's II Corps struck the Union flank from north and northeast. By mid-afternoon the Federals had been driven through Gettysburg and were holding on to high ground just south of the town. Lee was bringing up the rest of his army, while Meade was hurrying his own infantry to the scene.

Reynolds did not live to see much of it. He rode forward to get the Iron Brigade lined up against Hill's advancing infantry, in the woods and fields of a farm owned by a man named McPherson, and some Confederate sharpshooter in Mr. McPherson's barn drew a bead on him and shot him dead. Reynolds might have had command of the Army of the Potomac—it appears that the job was definitely offered to him not long after the battle of Chancellorsville—but he did not want it because he believed the War Department interfered with the army's commander too much; he said so and the job went to Meade, and now Reynolds was killed in the opening moments of the battle he had helped to bring on.

Command of the I Army Corps passed temporarily to the senior division commander, Major General Abner Doubleday, and as fast as fresh Union troops came up Doubleday fed them into action. A Confederate attack south of the Chambersburg road was beaten back sharply, and a Confederate brigade trying to advance through a railroad cut north of the road was broken up with heavy loss; but Hill had more men than Doubleday had and he kept piling them in relentlessly, and while the Federals held their ground tenaciously, they suffered fearful casualties. Before the day ended the Iron Brigade had been wrecked, one of its regiments having lost 80 per cent of its numbers, and the whole I Corps had been so badly mangled that it was never again really effective as a combat force. During the following winter it was broken up, with its survivors distributed among other corps.

Until noon and past, the Union I Corps managed to

hold its ground. Then a new pressure developed—a powerful battle line of Confederate infantry, marching south from the general direction of Carlisle: Major General Robert Rodes's division of Ewell's II Corps, coming in on the Federal right flank as neatly as if it had all been planned in advance.

Federal reinforcements came up just in time, Howard's XI Corps hurrying up from the south on the double in response to the messages Reynolds sent out before he died. Howard conferred briefly with Doubleday, took general command, by seniority, of all the troops present, planted one of his brigades as reserve on Cemetery Hill, the high ground just south of Gettysburg, and sent the rest of his corps into the open country north of town to meet Rodes's attack. For a time the situation was stabilized, and an enlarged battle rolled and crashed across the Pennsylvania countryside, the two Federal corps making a line that ran north and south along the ground of the morning's fight and then bent eastward at right angles in an improvised line that could hold temporarily but was by no means strong enough to meet any additional pressure.

Additional pressure came at once. Among the odd chances that combined to bring about a major battle at Gettysburg was the fact that Lee's order for a concentration of the army brought his troops into the Gettysburg area at the precise times and places where they could do the Federals the most harm. Now it was another of Ewell's divisions, commanded by the dour fighting man Major General Jubal Early, hurrying westward from York, that found itself coming into battle when and where it was

The first Federal infantry to reach the battlefield was Major General John F. Reynolds' I Army Corps. Meade had ordered Reynolds forward to determine whether Gettysburg was a suitable place for a battle and gave him temporary control of the III and XI Corps besides his own. Reynolds had his men relieve Buford's overmatched cavalry and opened a hot fight along Seminary Ridge and astride a railway cutting north of the Chambersburg road; he ordered the other infantry forward and sent word to Meade that Gettysburg was a good place to fight. Having done this, he rode forward to arrange his battle line and was shot dead by a Confederate sharpshooter. An enlisted man who rode with him as his orderly said later that he had seen many men killed in the war but that he never saw a man die as quickly as did Reynolds. Apparently the general was lifeless before his body struck the ground.

Death of Reynolds / Gettysburg

most needed. It struck Howard's exposed right flank and lapped over into the area behind him, and Early ordered a vigorous advance. Howard's men had had all they could do to stave off the attack from the north. Before this new assault they were helpless.

By the oddest chance Lee himself reached the scene shortly before this happened. He had started eastward from Chambersburg in the morning, with Longstreet's corps preparing to take the road behind him; hearing the sound of Hill's battle, Lee had spurred on ahead, and he rode up to Hill's field headquarters and got a size-up of the situation. He concluded at once that this fight ought not to be pressed any farther just now. He had no idea where the rest of Meade's army was, less than half of his own army was on the scene, and it seemed to him that it would be rash to bring on a finish fight until he had all of his own forces in hand and knew where the bulk of the opposing force might be. He told Hill not to press the offensive—and just then the arrival of Early's division caught the Federals in the flank. Ewell's third division was not far away, Long-

For the most part, the story of the July 1 fighting at Gettysburg is a story of unrelieved defeat for the Federal troops, but during the morning hours there were moments of triumph. One of these came when Southern troops tried to advance down an unfinished railroad cutting north of the Chambersburg road and were overpowered and compelled to surrender. The artist who made this sketch wrote that he followed the description of a Union Officer who was engaged here and who said that Brigadier General James J. Archer's Confederate brigade was the one that ran into trouble; the artist himself was doubtful that the capture took place here. Apparently Archer himself was taken prisoner south of the Chambersburg road, but his brigade—which was in Major General Harry Heth's division of the III Corps—did lose some 500 men captured in the first day's fight and the railroad cutting was the only place where any appreciable number of Confederates were taken prisoner on that day.

street's troops were on the road and would be up in a few hours; here was what looked very much like a decisive victory taking shape under the smoke clouds to the north and east—and Lee instantly reversed himself and ordered a general offensive by everybody in sight.

So the battle flared up anew and the Federals were overwhelmed. Howard's corps was simply swamped, and though valiant rear-guard elements bought as much time as they could, the corps as a whole had to retreat pell-mell through Gettysburg to temporary safety on Cemetery Hill. When these men retreated, Doubleday's men could not hold their ground because the exultant Confederates were storming in behind them and attacking them furiously from in front as well. After a bitter last-ditch struggle around the Lutheran seminary, these Federals took off for Gettysburg, ran through the disorderly town (full of battle smoke and lost soldiers, bullets flying in every direction, victors and defeated mingling in a confused, bewildering turmoil), and made their way to Cemetery Hill and the long ridge that ran south from it, aligning their right flank with Howard's left.

While all this was happening, Reynolds' messages had reached Meade, who had his headquarters fifteen miles to the south, and Meade at once acted to pull his army together. Learning that Reynolds had been killed, Meade sent Major General Winfield S. Hancock, commander of the II Corps, hurrying into Gettysburg with orders to assume general command there and to determine whether Gettysburg was a suitable place for the all-out fight with Lee that Meade was determined to fight sooner or later.

Hancock came up just as the beaten Federals were assembling on the high ground south of Gettysburg. He seems to have had a brief dispute with Howard, who ranked him and who did not see why he himself should not continue to command this part of Meade's army, but Hancock was a burly, energetic man who took this in his stride. He established his own authority, got the broken fragments of the I and XI Corps into position as best he could, sent word to Meade that Gettysburg would be a very good place to have a battle, and settled down to hold on until the rest of the army came up.

If what Hancock feared was a renewal late that afternoon of the Confederate assault, he was agreeably disappointed, because the assault was not renewed. Confederate survivors argued about this for years to come—indeed, the argument is still going on, in the books—and Lee's admirers have always asserted that a great chance was missed because General Ewell failed to follow up the day's triumph with a sweeping assault on the disorganized Federals who were taking refuge on Cemetery Hill. Certainly the Federals had been roughly handled—between them, the two corps had lost close to half of their strength and it took time to get the fugitives sorted out and put into position for a new fight—and if Ewell's men could have followed up their victory by surging on through the town and storming the insecure defenses on the heights,

When he learned that Reynolds had been killed, General
Meade sent Major General Winfield S. Hancock forward
to take charge at Gettysburg. Hancock reached the scene
early in the afternoon of July 1, just in time to see the overmatched Unionists driven away from their positions north
and west of town. He determined that the high ground
below Gettysburg—Culp's Hill, Cemetery Hill, and the
long stretch of Cemetery Ridge running south to the Round
Tops—could and should be held. He organized what troops
were at hand to hold this ground and sent word of his decision to Meade, who promptly ordered the rest of the army to
Gettysburg and came on himself, reaching the scene around
midnight. Here is a studio picture of Hancock; "Hancock
the Superb," newspaper writers called him, one of the dominant actors in the Union army's greatest victory.

a momentous battle might have been won. In the years since July 1, 1863, a great deal of criticism has descended on General Dick Ewell.

Most of the criticism is undeserved. It is true enough that for half an hour or so after the first Federals reached the high ground, the Federal army was not in good shape to stand off a vigorous attack, but it is mortally hard to see how such an attack could have been made. Ewell's men just were not in shape to make it on the heels of the Federal retreat. Rodes's division had suffered extremely heavy losses, Early's was temporarily disorganized by the pursuit through town, Ewell's third division was just beginning to come up, and during the half hour or so when the opportunity was really at its best, an attack was not quite practicable. Later in the day it might indeed have been made, but by that time the Federals probably were able to hold their ground. They held a strong defensive position, reinforcements were on their way, and it is probably true that by the time the Confederates were ready to launch an assault the opportunity had passed.

As a matter of fact, Lee was on the scene, and if he had felt that an assault was in order he could have ordered it. He did not do so; nor did he join in the criticism of Ewell after the battle. He did indicate that he believed something, somehow, had been missed when he said, long afterward, that if he had had Stonewall Jackson with him, he would have won the battle of Gettysburg; but to say that Ewell was not Stonewall's equal was not necessarily to criticize him. Nobody else was, either.

In any case, when night came the armies stayed where they were, Federals on the hills south of Gettysburg, Confederates arrayed on the rolling country to the north and west. For whatever it was worth, the town itself was in Confederate possession, but this fight was not waged for possession of a town. It had begun as an almost accidental collision between two armies, it had continued because sheer force of circumstances made it impossible to break it off, and it was actually fought for possession of control over the future of America.

Three

SECOND DAY: FIGHTING BY COMPULSION

On the morning of July 2 General Robert E. Lee appeared to be on the crest of the wave. He had won a smashing victory, he had his army in hand now, and there was good reason to suppose that he would complete the triumph today. By nightfall Confederate independence might well be very near.

Certainly the Confederate rank and file believed so. They had been fighting the Army of the Potomac, off and on, for two years now and except for the stand-off fight at Antietam in the early fall of 1862 they had won every engagement. In December they had rebuffed the Yankees at Fredericksburg so handily that half of the Southern army did not even have to get into action. In May, at Chancellorsville, they had inflicted an ignominious defeat on foes who outnumbered them at least two to one. Now, invading the enemy heartland, they had won the first engagement decisively, inflicting ruinous losses and driving the Northerners away from their defensive positions. There seemed to be every reason to believe that the next twenty-four hours might see the job finished once and for all.

Yet the situation was not as rosy as it looked. Winning the first encounter, Lee had in fact put himself in a position where he would have to fight at a disadvantage. For the first time in this war the Federal army—larger than the Army of Northern Virginia, as was always the case— was able to stand on the defensive on its own soil. Lee would have to force the fighting all the way.

The pressure of time was on him and not on his opponent. Lee could not stand his ground and wait for the Federals to attack; living off the country as it was, his army had to keep moving, and unless it went back to Virginia immediately, tacitly admitting that the whole invasion had failed, it could not move until it had beaten the Army of the Potomac. It could not wait for the enemy to put himself in a false position and then pounce upon an exposed fragment, and it could not let the enemy wear himself out in a fruitless assault and then strike a crippling counterblow. It had to fight right there and right then—on the enemy's terms.

Furthermore, there was no possibility for the kind of maneuvering at which Lee excelled. Jeb Stuart was still not there, and without him Lee could not put his army on the march; if he did, he had no way to tell what he might run into. General Longstreet, stoutest of his corps commanders, had this impressed upon him as this day began.

Longstreet came up to Lee's headquarters in advance of his corps, which had camped for the night a few miles to the west and would be up fairly soon. Longstreet listened to the accounts of the first day's fighting, took in as much of the general situation as could be seen from the ridge where the Lutheran seminary was, and then proposed that Lee move around to the south, circling past the Union left flank and striking for Meade's rear. Logically, this was the correct move, and it was in fact what Meade feared Lee would do; but Lee could not do it because under the circumstances it would have been wildly rash. He did not know where all of Meade's army was, he had no way to find out, and if he tried a flank march now he might run into a ruinous ambush.

He had at last learned where Stuart was—he had got his cavalry corps up in the neighborhood of Carlisle, miles to the north, where it was not needed at all, and he and his horsemen would be on hand tomorrow; but Lee needed him today, this morning, and he was not going to have him. Without him he could not make the move Longstreet was urging, and he answered Longstreet in the only way he could answer: "No. The enemy is there and I am going to fight him there."

Lee outlined his battle plan without delay. He would strike at Meade's flanks, trying to crush both ends of his line simultaneously. To be sure, the Federal position was powerful, but Lee's army had the habit of victory, and Lee seems to have been confident that it could sweep everything before it, once it struck with all its might. He told Longstreet to lead his corps down behind Seminary Ridge and prepare to attack to the eastward. At the same time Ewell would assault the high ground that had not been taken the night before; and Hill, in the center of the line, would lend a hand in either of these assaults or move forward on his own, as circumstances might indicate. The fighting was to begin as soon as Longstreet got his men into position.

It took several hours to do this, and after the war many Southerners bitterly criticized Longstreet, saying that he sulked because his own plan had been rejected and complaining that he could have moved much more rapidly if his heart had been in it. Sulky, Longstreet undoubtedly was, but he does seem to have moved as rapidly as possible—after all, it took time to get 12,000 infantry men off the road, move them cross-lots through wooded country, and then shake them out into a battle line ready to make a co-ordinated charge. It might be noted that to the end of his life Lee did not criticize Longstreet's behavior on this day. In any case, Longstreet was ready by midafternoon or thereabouts and the great battle of the second day began.

Meade's army was fully confident. For the first time it was fighting on its own soil, and every soldier realized that the job now was to hold on and let the enemy force the fighting; all in all, the men believed that they were going to win this one, and if they drew no especial inspiration from Meade's leadership that did not matter. From first to last, the generals who led this army owed more to the private soldiers than the soldiers owed to them. The men carried within themselves whatever the mysterious quality is that enables a soldier to surpass himself on the battlefield.

The Federal position was strong. Hancock had been right when he told Meade that this was a good place to fight a battle, and Meade—who had reached the field around midnight on the night of July 1 — fully agreed once he had studied the layout.

The Federal right was posted on Culp's Hill, a massive, wooded height southeast of Gettysburg. This was held by the XII Corps under Major General Henry W. Slocum, and on the corps' left, occupying slightly lower ground that swung westward just south of Gettysburg to the high ground of Cemetery Hill, were elements from the shattered I Corps. (Meade was not satisfied with the way Doubleday handled the corps and appointed Major General John Newton to replace him.) Cemetery Hill and the high ground around it was held by Howard and his XI Corps, with artillery posted to sweep the approaches. South from this strong point went Cemetery Ridge, a more or less open stretch whose height diminished as it ran south, and here the II Corps, under Hancock, was stationed, with General Dan Sickles' III Corps on its left.

Major General George Sykes and the V Corps were in immediate reserve, ready to reinforce any part of the left, and coming up from the rear was the reliable VI Corps led by Major General John Sedgwick. It had been far to the east when the order to bring the army together went out, and it was now making a tremendous forced march under a blistering July sun. It probably would not be ready for much action today, but it would be a powerful reserve in case anything went wrong.

The army's left was supposed to be anchored on rocky heights a couple of miles south of Cemetery Hill — Little Round Top, a craggy knob at the foot of Cemetery Ridge, and Big Round Top half a mile to the south. But General Sickles, who held the left, suspected that the Confeder-

Lee's major effort in the battle of July 2 was a furious attack
by Lieutenant General James Longstreet's I Corps on the
Union left, which Major General Dan Sickles, commander
of the III Corps, had advanced to the Emmitsburg road, the
peach orchard, and a wheat field—a salient jutting out a mile
in advance of the position on Little Round Top and lower
Cemetery Ridge which Sickles had been ordered to hold.
Longstreet's men struck this salient with tremendous power,
breaking the defending force and threatening to destroy the
entire Union position. This unfinished sketch by an artist
catches one of the desperate moments when a Union battery, in the center of the picture, supported by infantry, tries
desperately to hold the ground in the face of a Confederate
attack coming from the right and right-center of the picture.

ates were about to attack him and believed he would be in a stronger position if he moved forward to elevated ground along the Emmitsburg road, half a mile or more to the west of the ground he had been ordered to occupy. He asked for Meade's permission to move forward, failed to get it, and then moved out on his own hook, posting one of his two divisions on the Emmitsburg road facing west and the other one in a peach orchard and a wheat field facing almost south. He had no sooner got them established there than Longstreet opened his attack.

Some of the worst fighting of the battle came on the afternoon of July 2 when Longstreet's men drove Federal defenders out of a tangle of rocky ground known as the Devil's Den. Here a battlefield sketch of the beginning of this Federal defeat catches the sense of confusion that possessed this disordered part of a desperate field.

Longstreet was deliberate in getting into position, but when he did strike he hit with great power. He was fighting with only two of his divisions today, under Major Generals Lafayette McLaws and John B. Hood; his third, Pickett's, had been doing rear-guard duty around Chambersburg, and although it was on its way to Gettysburg, it would not be ready for action until tomorrow—when, as a matter of fact, there would be more than enough grim work for it to do. Longstreet was putting between 12,000 and 14,000 men into action and he struck Dan Sickles' corps with overwhelming force.

The defects of Sickles' chosen position were revealed at once, and many good Union soldiers paid with their lives for this general's lack of battlefield savvy. From the southwest Longstreet's artillery pounded the angle of Sickles' line, and while Hood's division swarmed in against the southern face of the line, McLaws' division attacked the western face. In effect, Sickles was struck on three sides at once, and his undersized army corps was swamped. Sickles himself was carried off the field with one leg shattered by a cannon ball, and Confederate General Hood was disabled by a painful wound in the arm; but the fury of the Confederate attack and the tenacity of the Federal resistance were not diminished, and the battle rose to an unendurable intensity.

Meade ordered one of Hancock's divisions to come to the rescue; then, when the Federals were driven out of wheat field and peach orchard and tried stubbornly to hold on in a formless jumble of rocks and scrub trees south of the wheat field—the soldiers called this place "the Devil's Den," and they named it well—Meade told General Sykes to bring the V Corps into action.

Sykes's men were veterans, and in their ranks was a division of regulars, who gave a special flavor of disciplined toughness to the entire corps. The regulars were shock troops fit for any emergency, but the whole left of Meade's battle line had come unraveled and to stitch it together again under fire was almost impossible. The first essential was to find a secure anchorage for the left flank, and the only possible spot for this was Little Round Top, the hill which Sickles had so blithely abandoned when he moved forward to what he thought was a better position. Hood's troops now were in the Devil's Den, moving on for Little Round Top. If they took it, Meade's entire position on Cemetery Ridge would be untenable and the battle would end in a smashing Confederate victory.

Apparently there was nothing to keep them from doing it, because the only Federals on Little Round Top just then were members of a Signal Corps detachment. Luckily, however, Meade had sent one of his ablest staff officers, Major General G. K. Warren of the Engineers, down to the left to see what was needed and Warren went to the top of the rocky little hill to survey the situation. What he saw was an advancing line of Confederates, coming out of the trees and shrubs at the edge of Devil's Den and splashing across a little creek that flowed past the foot of Little Round Top, and they carried final defeat for the Union cause on their bayonets. Warren galloped off pell-mell for reinforcements.

In the Devil's Den and on Little Round Top the soldiers protected themselves as well as they could by piling rocks into
crude breastworks. The photograph above, taken immediately after the battle, shows a lifeless Confederate sharpshooter in one of the niches in Devil's Den; the two photos
on the next page show Union defenses on Little Round Top.

By good luck he ran into one of Sykes's advancing brigades whose commander recognized him and knew that any orders Warren might give him would come with Meade's authority, and when Warren told him to get his men to the top of the hill he obeyed promptly. Next Warren found a battery of field artillery, and by dint of enormous exertion—the slope was steep and rocky, and there was no road—the men got these guns up to the crest . . . and by the narrowest margin imaginable the Confederate attack was beaten off. Then additional Union troops were sent farther south to take possession of Big Round Top, and in the end Meade had a solid anchorage for his left. But as the Duke of Wellington remarked after the battle of Waterloo, it had been a damned near thing.

The crisis was by no means over. The Round Tops were at last secure, but the whole area between them and Hancock's position on the upper end of Cemetery Ridge was a no man's land. Longstreet's attack had not yet lost its impetus, a division from Hill's corps was coming into action from the west, on Longstreet's left, and bits and pieces of three Federal army corps were eddying about under heavy fire trying to find a rallying point. At one place nothing but an improvised line of Federal cannon, devoid of any infantry help whatever, held the ground; at another a Confederate charge was beaten back when Hancock called on one of the army's best regiments, the 1st Minnesota, to make a counterattack all unsupported. This prevented a Confederate penetration that might have wrecked everything, but the 1st Minnesota was all but destroyed, losing more than 80 per cent of its men. A little farther north, some of Hill's soldiers seized a rank of guns on the very crest of Cemetery Ridge, but Meade was getting reinforcements to the scene and these Southerners at last had to retreat. When darkness at last descended, the Union left was holding its ground and apparently could continue to do so, but the men had never had to fight any harder than they fought this afternoon.

At the other end of the line, the extreme Union right, the fighting had been equally severe. Ewell's men had gone valiantly up the steep wooded slopes of Culp's Hill; not only had the ground not permitted effective use of the dominant Federal artillery, but Meade had also had to take troops from this hill to buttress the line on Cemetery Ridge, and his defense here was under strength. The Federals were well dug in, however, and they were good men—they belonged to General Slocum's XII Corps— and they beat off four consecutive attacks without giving ground. But if the Confederates could not quite get to the crest of the hill, they were of no mind to give up, and when darkness came they held a ragged line halfway up the hill, overlapping the Union right and in excellent position to drive past it into the Union rear. It was as certain as anything could be that they would renew their offensive as soon as morning came.

Even the fighting on Culp's Hill did not complete the story. Between Culp's Hill and Cemetery Hill, facing north toward the town of Gettysburg, there was a saddle of higher ground held by assorted Federals, and as dusk came on, the Confederate General Early took his division up a ravine and sent battle lines swinging up the slope against this part of the Union line. There was desperate fighting here, the half-light of evening all clogged

These two contrasting sketches supposedly depict the same part of the battle on the second day—the union repulse of the Confederate drive to take Little Round Top and destroy Meade's left. One picture is of the traditional "picture-book" school, grotesquely unreal, showing orderly ranks of Union troops advancing behind a general who rides valiantly in front waving a flag. The other picture comes much closer to realism, showing the Confederates advancing up the littered hillside by twos and threes and squads, taking cover behind rocks and trees, fighting in a smoky fog in which no parade-ground battle lines were ever visible.

with blinding layers of powder smoke, and although the defenders near Culp's Hill beat their assailants off, several Louisiana regiments farther west broke through entirely and overran the XI Corps artillery on Cemetery Hill, driving one of the XI Corps infantry brigades away and threatening to break Meade's line right in half. But the Confederates who attacked here were up against the cruel handicap that operated against Lee's men throughout the last two days at Gettysburg: whenever they got into a Union position they moved farther and farther away

from their own army and closer and closer to the Union's reserve forces, so that it was impossible to exploit their success. Now, as full darkness was coming in, and the fighting lines could be marked only by the pin-point sparkles of flame from infantry muskets, Hancock sent a brigade over to the rescue and it struck the Louisianians with paralyzing force, drove them back to their own lines, and restored the situation for Meade.

The two hills known as Little Round Top and Big Round Top were not actually very high or imposing, but they dominated the nearby terrain just enough to compel any army that wanted to possess Cemetery Ridge to take them first. This scene, taken shortly after the battle, shows Little Round Top on the left, with the larger hill on the right.

This view of Little Round Top and the two views on the
next page show the craggy rocks and the scrubby trees that
marked this part of the field.

One of the axioms of military science in the 1860s was that artillery alone could not hold a position; it had to have infantry in support. There was a time on the Union left, late on July 2, when this axiom had to be disregarded. Sickles' line had been pulverized, and although the Round Tops were being held, the Confederates threatened to sweep in north of them and swamp the disorganized defenders of the southern end of Cemetery Ridge. A hastily assembled line of cannon staved off the assault until infantry reinforcements could reach the scene. Here the artist sketches Captain John Bigelow's 9th Massachusetts battery dashing forward into action.

The furious nature of the fighting on the Union left late on July 2 is indicated by this sketch showing Union artillerists withdrawing a piece by hand. All the horses have been killed, and if the piece is to be saved the gunners themselves have to do the work. This method of withdrawal had one thin advantage. It was easy to stop and fire a round at the oncoming foe, because there was no team to be unhitched and no caisson to detach.

The distinguished sketch artist Edwin Forbes made this drawing of the goings-on atop Culp's Hill on the afternoon of July 2, 1863. No sketch artist could quite catch all of it, and this one is slightly formal, stiff, and unreal; yet the ominous battle smoke does ride above the log breastworks, and if the arriving reinforcements have a picture-book air, there is at least the feeling that they are about to step into something violent and dreadful . . . which is the key to the happenings on that hilltop on that sultry July afternoon.

Butler's battery gone into position. — ARW.

ABOVE: In the fight to save Cemetery Ridge on July 2, Meade's chief of artillery sent in batteries wherever he could find them. Here Lieutenant John Butler's Battery G, 2nd U.S. Artillery, from the VI Corps, in reserve, is driven forward to take part in the fight.

RIGHT: Lee's army attacked savagely on the afternoon of July 2, Ewell striking Meade's right on Culp's Hill while Longstreet assailed his left in front of the Round Tops. Sickles, commanding Meade's III Corps, had unwisely advanced to hold a salient along the Emmitsburg road; his corps was routed and only the timely arrival of Sykes's V Corps, along with reinforcements from other parts of Meade's line, kept the entire left flank from being crushed. In the end, Culp's Hill and the Round Tops were held, a thrust at Cemetery Ridge by part of Hill's corps was beaten back, and an attack by Early, of Ewell's corps, on the ground between Culp's Hill and Cemetery Ridge was repulsed.

PICKETT

CHAMBERSBURG RD.

YORK RD.

SEMINARY RIDGE

HAGERSTOWN RD.

Gettysburg

RODES,
OF EWELL'S CORPS

EARLY

EWELL'S
II CORPS

CEMETERY
HILL

HILL'S III CORPS

HOWARD'S
XI CORPS

CULP'S
HILL

SLOCUM'S
XII CORPS

HANCOCK'S
II CORPS

LEE

CEMETERY RIDGE

BALTIMORE RD.

MEADE

McLAWS

PEACH
ORCHARD

*Federal line finally stabilized
from here to the Round Tops*

SEDGWICK'S
VI CORPS

LONGSTREET'S I CORPS

POSITION HELD
BY SICKLES'S
III CORPS

HOOD

WHEAT
FIELD

LITTLE
ROUND TOP

SYKES'S
V CORPS

ROCK CREEK

EMMITSBURG RD.

DEVIL'S DEN

N

PLUM RUN

ROUND TOP

TANEYTOWN RD.

Afternoon of July 2

Note: Elements of the shattered I Corps
were in line between Howard and Slocum,
and on Cemetery Ridge in support of Hancock

One Mile

palacios

The final Confederate offensive thrust of July 2 came at dusk in the form of a sharp assault on the XI Corps position on East Cemetery Hill and on the slightly lower ground running east from that spot to Culp's Hill. These two sketches, which are hardly more than the artist's shorthand but which do preserve something of the tension of violent action, show the Federal battery position and the charge of the Louisiana brigade which came close to seizing and holding this position.

The picture shows the rocky slopes and gloomy woods along the base of Little Round Top. Confederate troops from Longstreet's I Corps made a desperate assault which, if successful, would have destroyed Meade's battle line and given General Robert E. Lee a sweeping victory. Here is a glimpse of the desolate battleground, photographed just after the battle had ended and before the dead bodies had been buried.

Late that night, with a full moon shining down grotesquely through the smoke-stained air and the night all clamorous with the cries of wounded men calling for help—the July heat was a heavy burden, and the wounded men desperately wanted water—Meade held a council of war in the little farmhouse on the eastern slope of Cemetery Ridge that served as his headquarters. One after another his corps commanders made their reports: they had had a tremendous fight and losses had been frightful, but they believed they could hold their ground if Lee renewed the attack tomorrow. (To a man, they expected him to do so. They had seen enough of him by this time to know that he could be counted on to go on fighting as long as a chance of victory remained.)

Meade did not need to reflect very long. He had had his chief of staff prepare tentative plans for withdrawal, in case worse came to worst, but he had no intention of using them unless he had to, and although he had lost 20,000 men thus far he sensed that this fight was costing his opponent even more and he knew that his own cue was to stay where he was. He made up his mind to do the obvious thing—hold on, and if Lee did not attack, go over to the offensive—and he told one of Hancock's generals that he expected Lee to attack the Union center on July 3. When the general asked why he looked for this, Meade remarked that Lee had struck both flanks and failed: the center was the only objective left.

As it happened, the center—the ground along the

Veterans of the Civil War said that a battlefield could show no more hideous sight than the mangled corpses in front of a place that had been defended by close-range artillery fire, which tore human bodies as musketry could not do. Here is grim testimony to the truth of this statement. The photograph was made, apparently, on the Union left.

upper part of Cemetery Ridge, where the ridge joins
Cemetery Hill—was the strongest part of the Union line,
and that Meade should expect Lee to strike him there
showed that he had an intuitive understanding of the
compulsion under which the great Confederate general
was laboring at Gettysburg.

Late at night on July 2, after the dreadful fighting of the second day had come to an end, General Meade held a council
of war in his farmhouse headquarters on the reverse slope of
Cemetery Ridge. Here he found that his generals felt just as
he did—that the army should hold its ground and repel the
final assault that Lee would inevitably make next day. Orders
were issued accordingly. Afterward, some of Meade's politi-
cal enemies spread the story that he had prepared to retreat
and actually drew up orders for a withdrawal, but this was
eventually exposed as a false tale; among others, adherents
of General Sickles, who was being criticized for his unwise
advance in front of the Round Tops just before Longstreet's
assault struck him, tried to restore their general's reputation
by undermining Meade's.

. The Union position on East Cemetery Hill was retained, finally, when a brigade from Hancock's II Corps came over and drove the Confederates out of the ground they had seized among the guns. The artist who prepared this picture back in New York believed that the scene looked like this.

By sunset of July 2 the Federal position on the left was fairly well stabilized; much ground and many lives had been lost, but Longstreet's powerful attack had at least been contained, and reinforcements had been sent forward to replace the men who had fallen or who had been driven away. Here is a graphic sketch of the position as seen from Little Round Top as the afternoon was drawing to a close.

On the day after the battle ended, an artist made this sketch of relaxed Union soldiers behind their log-and-rock breast-works on the slopes and at the base of Culp's Hill, the anchor for the Union right.

Lee could not withdraw from this battle without admitting outright defeat, he could not simply hold his ground and wait for the Federals to come over to the offensive, and the armies were locked together too tightly to permit the kind of maneuver that Longstreet had called for. Lee was compelled to strike one more blow on July 3, and he had just strength enough for one more blow: Pick-ett's division had at last come up and could be used for the final stroke of Lee's offensive battle. Ewell's men, who had assaulted Culp's Hill so valiantly, had by no means fought themselves out. If Pickett, suitably reinforced by units from other commands, struck a hard blow at the center while Ewell renewed the assault on Culp's Hill, the day might well be won.

So it looked on the night of July 2, while soldiers from both armies wandered about the field looking for wounded comrades, and uneasy skirmishers kept up a spat-spat of rifle fire on the low ground beyond Culp's Hill. And what nobody quite noticed at the time was that Robert E. Lee was fighting this battle in a manner unlike any he had followed before. His army had become a superb instrument for finding and exploiting enemy weak spots, and over and over again it had won battles against superior numbers by behaving in that way. Now, for the first time, it was hitting the enemy's strong points; in effect, it was fighting Meade's way, not Lee's. Coming north of the Potomac, the Army of Northern Virginia had mislaid its old recipe for victory.

Four

THIRD DAY: CLIMAX

———————

*I*n a way the story of Gettysburg is the story of the country roads that come to the place. They were unpaved roads in 1863, white and dusty under the July sun, binding town to countryside, knitting the Pennsylvania townships together, unremarkable and unknown to fame; bearing now a strange traffic. Thousands of men tramped along them to meet what was waiting at the end of the last hard mile, stepping off the map altogether, stumbling painfully onward and winning a soldier's apotheosis on hills and fields that sandwiched three days of violence in between unbroken generations of peace to make the more perfect union the nation's elders had dreamed of.

The nation gained unity and an immortal legend because the soldiers followed these roads. What the soldiers themselves gained is not quite so clear, but now and then the haze of the dead years thins out and shows us a few of these young men and we are left with long thoughts. One young man we can get a look at was named

Wesley Culp. He was born in Gettysburg, in a house on Culp's Hill—his family gave its name to the place and had its home under the trees on top of it—and in his early teens Wesley Culp left home and went out into the world to seek his fortune. He settled somewhere in the upper Shenandoah Valley, and when the war came he considered himself a Virginian and enlisted in the Confederate army. He came back to Gettysburg as an infantryman in General Ewell's II Corps, and when the men of that corps tried to win the battle by capturing Culp's Hill he was in one of the assault waves. He was killed within a few yards of the house where he was born, and at your leisure you can try to appraise the ins and outs of his tragic fate.

Another soldier who comes in for a brief close-up is young Colonel Strong Vincent, who commanded a brigade of Union infantry in General Sykes's V Corps. On the night of July 1 he was leading his brigade north toward Gettysburg on a driving forced march, and the men were on the road long after night came. There was a bright moon, and when the brigade came to a little town, the regiments broke out their battle flags and set their bands playing, and in every doorway and shadowed yard there were girls waving and cheering. Colonel Vincent reined in his horse while the column went through the town, doffing his hat as the flags passed him, looking at the town and the girls and the soldiers, and to an aide he remarked that there could be a worse fate than to die fighting here in Pennsylvania with the flag overhead. . . .

Then he resumed the march along the road to Gettysburg: the long road white in the moonlight, with the small-town girls laughing and crying in the shadows and the young men waving and passing on. To the girls who had been nowhere and had all of life ahead of them, this was the first of all the roads on earth, and to many of the young men it was the last road of all—and to girls and boys alike, equally, it led to unutterable mystery. It was the last road for Strong Vincent, because the next afternoon, when General Warren rode desperately to find troops to hold Little Round Top, Colonel Vincent's brigade was one that was sent there, and Vincent lost his life in the way he had chosen, fighting on Pennsylvania soil under the national flag . . . defending a rocky hillock that had to be held if the union of the states was to survive.

Lee had come over the Chambersburg road from the west, riding up the long slope of South Mountain and then coming down to the clamorous plain with its great streaked blanket of battle smoke hiding the future and all its chances. Meade had come up the Emmitsburg road from the south to see the battle his advance guard had prepared for him, and they may have told him how the first Federal infantry, the Iron Brigade (wrecked now almost beyond repair), had left the road just below Gettysburg to go cross-lots over to Seminary Ridge, where Yankee cavalry was trying to hold off Confederate infantry. The Federal commander had sent the fife and drum corps to the head of the column to play the men into their last great fight, and it played "The Campbells Are Coming," the fifes shrilling out above the hard clatter of musket fire, the rattle of drums jarred off balance by the heavy concussion of artillery fire. . . . There had been hard fight-

ing that day of July 1, and harder fighting on July 2, and
now it was July 3 and time for this bloody business to
come to its climax.

The climax was approaching fast enough, but it was
not coming quite as Lee had planned. He would send
Pickett and his division against the Union center, with
good fighting brigades from Hill's and Longstreet's corps
to help out, making a charging column of somewhere
between 10,000 and 15,000 men; and when they struck
the center, Ewell would renew his assault on Culp's Hill,
and Stuart's cavalry—on hand at last, days late—would
curl far around the Union right and disrupt the Union
rear. It was a good plan, and it might well succeed; from
Lee down to the last private, the Army of Northern Virginia believed it was irresistible when it hit with all its
strength. But co-ordination was lacking, this third day of
July, and the timing was off.

It took time to get Pickett and the supporting troops
in position, and Ewell's men could not wait. They had
made an uneasy bivouac halfway up the slopes of Culp's
Hill, and when dawn came they inevitably renewed their
fight without waiting for further orders. General Slocum,
the Union commander whose lines included Culp's Hill,
had had to send half of his corps away the evening before
to help buttress the Union left, but he had got his men
back during the night and reinforcements were at hand,
and when the fighting flared up this morning he was
ready for it. It was savage while it lasted, but the Union
position was strong and Slocum's soldiers blistered the
aisles between the trees with deadly musket fire, and long
before the morning was over the Confederate assailants

had to give up and retreat to the plain below. The attack on the hill was over, once and for all, before Pickett's men were ready to begin.

So there was a strange hour of tense, uneasy quiet at noon on July 3. Destiny was taking its time. As the morning wore away the great battlefield became almost hushed. Off to the east the last sound of the assault on Culp's Hill died away. Down by the Round Tops, Devil's Den, and the peach orchard firing had ceased. There was a brief flare-up, once, west of the place where the national cemetery now lies, when Federal and Confederate skirmishers and gunners contested briefly for a barn between the lines which made a good hiding place for sharpshooters. This fight swelled to a brief fortissimo, the barn took fire and was burned, and then the unimportant struggle ended. A haunted quiet developed, with a sense that a fuse was inexorably burning toward a mine.

George Gordon Meade knew no better than anyone else what was going to happen. He was certain only that he was ready for it, whenever and wherever it might come, and that his army was equally ready.

The weather was almost unbearably hot today and Meade was weary. To him, at noon, came an invitation to lunch. Brigadier General John Gibbon, commanding a division in Hancock's corps, had a meal ready on the reverse slope of Cemetery Ridge no great distance from Meade's headquarters. Meade rode over and, with Gibbon and Hancock and several staff officers, lounged on the grass to eat boiled chicken and potatoes. (The chickens, as Gibbon remembered, were good enough but somewhat tough.) After lunch Meade went back to his headquarters. Hancock called a clerk and began to dictate an order regarding commissary arrangements. A little to the west, beyond the crest of the ridge, Union infantrymen sweltered helplessly. Some of them tried to rig shelter-tent halves so as to get a little shade.

And then, suddenly, the great tension snapped.

Down by the peach orchard one of the Confederate field guns was fired, the sharp clang of the discharge echoing across the still field, while a puffball of white smoke drifted lazily up toward the sky, and Federal artillerymen on Cemetery Ridge blinked and wondered what the Johnnies were up to now. There was a brief pause, then another gun in the same battery was fired . . . the signal Lee's army was waiting for. All along the Confederate line, out in the shallow open valley west of Cemetery Ridge, from the peach orchard to the rising ground directly west of Gettysburg, there were 140 Confederate cannon, and on the signal the gunners who had been lounging nearby jumped up and ran to their posts. There was a long ripple of movement; then every gun in the Confederate line went off, in one long rolling crash—the loudest noise, probably, that had ever been heard on the North American continent up to that moment. The most stupendous bombardment of the Civil War had begun.

General Hancock and General Gibbon and the staff officers ran to their posts, and a hurricane of solid shot and exploding shell swept across Cemetery Ridge. Meade had read Lee's intention accurately; there was going to be a smashing attack on the Federal center, and this bombardment was meant to cut the infantry line and to break up the supporting artillery, paving the way for the Confederate advance.

General Gibbon wrote after the battle that he and an aide went forward to his division's picket line, down the slope a hundred yards or so west of the crest of the ridge, to see what could be seen of Lee's army. Gibbon found that he could see practically nothing. The whole shallow valley, two miles from north to south and half a mile or more in width, was brim full of boiling, eddying smoke— black smoke rising from the ground like a sluggish cloud, white smoke above it, the whole shot through incessantly by stabbing flashes of flame from guns that could not be seen. The uproar was so heavy and continuous that Union gunners on Cemetery Ridge, opening fire in reply, could not hear the reports of their own guns.

Massive though it was, this bombardment did not quite do what Lee had hoped it would do. The Confederate gunners were firing just a little too high. The waiting Federal infantry suffered comparatively little. ("Comparatively" is the word to emphasize: the sound and fury were wholly terrifying, and when shell exploded among the rocky ledges they sent deadly fragments of stone whirring into the ranks of defenders who hugged the ground desperately.) The Federal artillery got it worse, but the heaviest metal of all fell on the far side of Cemetery Ridge, where wagon and ambulance trains were parked, non-combat details were in waiting, stragglers of high and low degree had taken refuge, and general officers had their headquarters. The far slope which should have been so safe became briefly the most dangerous spot on the battlefield as shell came skimming over the crest to break among people who could not see the firing line. The stragglers, wagon trains, and military stand-bys in general broke for cover, and Meade found it impossible to carry on headquarters business in a little farm house that was continually being pierced by cannon balls. He moved, before long, to General Slocum's headquarters, farther east. While the bombardment lasted, General Gibbon, walking up and down in advance of the front line, found that he could stand erect without undue risk; actually he was much safer than the commanding general back at the supposedly secure headquarters.

No one really knows how long the great bombardment lasted, and the estimates (made by various men who lived through it) ran all the way from thirty minutes to two hours. It did end at last, as the Confederate stock of ready ammunition began to run low; so the Confederate fire faded, and the answering fire of the Union gunners died down as well, and slowly the great smoke bank lifted from the valley and men could see again.

Along Hancock's defensive line on the ridge Union soldiers looked to the woods that fringed the opposite ridge a mile to the west, and as the guns fell silent they could see a long ripple of movement, and men with rifles and flags stepped out into the open. The Federals saw, knew that the real test lay not far ahead, and muttered to one another:

"Here they are. Here comes the infantry."

Military men then had, and still have, a succinct expression: infantry is the Queen of Battles. Cavalry was very useful, and there were many jobs where powerful artillery was essential, but when the final showdown came the foot soldier carrying a rifle was the important figure. The big guns had done what they could; now it was the infantry that would settle matters.

The open hollow between the ridges was the great valley of the shadow of death, and when the smoke drifted up and spun away into misty fragments it was as if a curtain had gone up to reveal the stage of some terrible unimaginable theater. The Federal soldiers on the eastern ridge looked west; they were veterans and they had been in many battles, but what they saw now took their breath away. Some of them had seventy-five years yet to live and some of them had no more than ten minutes, but until they died they remembered the scene that now presented itself. There it was, for the last time in this war, perhaps for the last time anywhere, the fearful pageantry and color of war in the old style, beautiful and majestic and hideous; fighting men lined up in double and triple ranks, a solid mile from flank to flank, slashed red flags overhead, sunlight glinting off polished musket barrels — the flower of Lee's army coming forward, unhurried, for the great test that would determine whether there would hereafter be one nation or two between Canada and the Rio Grande . . . and whether Americans on American soil could continue to own other men and women, or be owned by them, as cattle and horses are owned.

The flower of Lee's army: 15,000 men, or perhaps a slightly smaller number, coming along with Pickett's division as the spearhead. Out of the trees and the shadows they came, and when they reached the open they paused and dressed their lines with parade-ground formality, as if they proposed to go about this business of crushing the Yankee host with a flourish in high style, pride and courage blending into arrogance and dauntless confidence. The ranked Confederate cannon were all silent as the infantry passed through, and on Cemetery Ridge the Union guns also were silent, and it was as if both armies waited to savor the war's supreme moment of drama.

The advancing Confederates had nearly a mile to go, and the odds were against them. Tough General Longstreet, who had urged Lee to swing off around the Union left to strike for the unprotected rear, did not think this attack could possibly succeed, and when Pickett rode up to him to say that the ranks were all formed and to ask if he should begin the charge, Longstreet was unable to put the order into words and could only bow his head in a choked gesture of command. These men were going to march uphill to strike the Union line where it was strongest, and they would be a perfect target. Furthermore, if they themselves were the flower of Lee's army, the men they were about to fight were the flower of Meade's army—Hancock's II Corps, mostly, with unbroken elements from the shattered I Corps, and with the powerful VI Corps available for use if reinforcements were needed. After the war Longstreet said that he had warned Lee that "no fifteen thousand men ever arrayed for battle can take that position," and whether he actually said it or just thought afterward that he should have said it, his appraisal stands. The thing just could not be done.

But the way it was tried still commands attention.

The great charge actually began in silence, as if the two armies consciously willed a lull while the long lines

were carefully dressed. The Confederate guns could not
fire while the infantrymen were passing through their
line, and most of the waiting Federal cannon had used
their long-range ammunition in the earlier artillery duel
and had to wait until the attackers came close; and the
troops were not yet within effective musket range. So the
long lines came forward, brimming up to the long diago-
nal of the Emmitsburg road, crossing it, and pausing once
more to perfect the dress. Then they moved on again,
and if the waiting Federals looked closely they could
have seen a Confederate officer who held his sword high
over his head, with his black felt hat on the lifted point
of it as a guide for his brigade — Brigadier General Lewis
Armistead, who was coming over the valley to meet death
and an old friend.

One of the most moving things about this tragic Civil
War was the fact that so many of the ranking officers
on both sides were close personal friends of the officers
whom they had to fight. Before the war the regular army
had been comparatively small, and everybody knew
everybody else, bound together in a closed professional
circle whose intimacy went back to the parade ground
and classrooms at West Point and continued through service at isolated little army posts all up and down the west
and along the coasts. When the nation broke in half and
went to war over it, some of these army officers remained
in Federal service and others took service with the Confederacy; and the war flung them cruelly against each
other, so that a general going into battle might very well
find himself confronting his closest friend. And General
Armistead illustrated this point perfectly.

General Hancock personally directed the spirited defense of the Union center, and at the climactic moment the scene may have looked something like this, making due allowances for the artist's trick of making things seem more orderly than they really were. Hancock, who was desperately wounded a few moments later, is on his horse in the left center; directly above him, his old friend Armistead, hat on sword, may be seen running forward to take possession of a Union gun.

Back in the spring of 1861, when the Union seemed to be dissolving and the officers of the old army were choosing their sides, there was a farewell party one evening in the officers' quarters of a little army post outside of what was then the little California town of Los Angeles. The man who gave the party was Captain Winfield Scott Hancock, and the guests of honor were fellow officers who were resigning their commissions in order to enter the army of the Southern Confederacy; among these was another captain, Lewis Armistead, who was one of Hancock's intimates. Late in the evening one of the officers' wives sang "Kathleen Mavourneen," that haunted song of a long parting—"It may be for years and it may be forever"—and then the party broke up and Armistead came over to shake hands with Hancock. Tears were in his eyes, and as he shook Hancock's hand Armistead said: "Goodbye—you never can know what this has cost me." Then he went away, and he and Hancock had not seen each other again. Now Armistead was leading the spearhead of Pickett's charge up Cemetery Ridge, and waiting for him at the crest was his old friend Hancock, with the shotted guns all around him.

When the Confederates formed their lines just before beginning to advance, they had designated a "little clump of trees" on Cemetery Ridge as their objective. It was a wholly unremarkable little grove, hardly big enough for a family to have a picnic in, and it had open fields all around it, with a low fence of stones and rails running along the western side. It lay on the skyline as a good landmark, right in the center of Hancock's line. Here was the spot Pickett's men were to hit, and as the long lines swung across the Emmitsburg road the flanking elements began to move in toward the center so that the entire mass could strike the selected place with maximum impact.

But at about the time the Southerners crossed the

road they began to have trouble. Much of Hancock's artillery might be out of action, waiting for close range, but when the attackers crossed the road they came within reach of the infantry's muskets, and these were the deadliest weapons of all. The field guns were frightening and under certain circumstances they could be devastating, but in the long run, battles were decided by musket fire and so it was here. As Pickett's men advanced, the right wing of the charging column had to cross an open space beyond which there was a brigade of Vermont infantry, and this infantry moved forward a hundred yards or so, swung to its right, caught the end of the Confederate line in flank and opened a killing fire that shattered the flank and sent the survivors crowding off toward the center. At the same time a long rank of reserve artillery, posted to the south of Hancock's infantry, began to fire obliquely down the length of the Confederate ranks, adding to the carnage. The right end of the assaulting column was crippled before it got to close quarters.

At the northern end of the line there was a similar story. Some Ohio troops had worked their way forward, like the Vermonters farther south, and these caught the Confederate left flank with a shockingly effective fire. Along the low stone wall facing the Confederates on this part of the field were Union soldiers armed with smooth-bore muskets in place of the rifled pieces that were standard equipment; but the range now was so close that the smooth-bores (charged with buckshot, they were today, usually with an overload) could have full effect, and the Confederates were under terrible fire from two sides.

The most famous and unremarkable grove in North America is probably the "little clump of trees" on Cemetery Ridge at Gettysburg. This grove stood at about the center of Meade's line, and when Lee ordered an assault on the Union center on July 3 his troops were told to march toward the clump of trees, which made a first-rate landmark. Here is the grove as it looks today.

Then the Union artillery got into the action again. There were plenty of guns here, off a few hundred yards to the north of the little clump of trees, and if they had used up their long-range ammunition, they had plenty of canister, and now they got off a furious blast. (Canister was the gunners' close-range ammunition; a charge of canister consisted simply of a tin can full of lead slugs somewhat smaller than golf balls. When the gun was fired, the tin can disintegrated and the slugs went out in an expanding cloud, like a charge fired from a monstrously over-sized sawed-off shotgun. Within 200 yards this weapon was murderous beyond belief.) When these guns were fired, men who saw it all said that the advancing Confederates disappeared in a boiling cloud of dust and smoke, in which knapsacks and muskets and horrible fragments of human bodies were tossed high in the air; one Federal soldier remembered that there came from this part of the field a strange sound that was like an agonized gasp of pain coming from hundreds of throats. No one seems to have remembered hearing any cheers from either side. One soldier recalled only "a vast mournful roar" that seemed to rise from the entire field.

Thus, as the great charge drew near to its objective, both its flanks had been broken. (Flanking fire was especially deadly, because the line that was being flanked could not make any reply to it and was itself utterly vulnerable; fire that came slicing along the length of an infantry line simply could not miss, and no troops could stand it very long.) Longstreet, looking on from the rear, saw what was happening and remarked to a British observer who was standing beside him that the attack was going to fail.

But it had not failed yet, and if the flanks of the Confederate line crumbled, the center was strong. It built up its strength now, in front of the memorable clump of trees. (The trees are still there, protected by an iron fence, all set off with monuments and plaques.) As they came in close—

whites-of-the-eyes range, at last—the Confederates halted. Standing, kneeling, or lying at full length, they opened their own rifle fire on the Federals. An infantry attack in the Civil War rarely involved an unbroken run forward followed by hand-to-hand work with the bayonet. The object usually was to try to build up an overpowering rifle fire at close range, gaining superior fire power at the point

A low stone wall topped by fence rails ran along the front and sides of the clump of trees and offered a good defensive position for Union infantry. In the ground shown in this picture, extremely quiet and peaceful-looking today, thousands of men struggled desperately at the great climax of the battle on July 3, when Major General George Pickett's charge reached this point, hung on there for a moment, and then broke up in defeat.

of contact. Even with their broken flanks, the Confederates were accomplishing this here, and along the low wall that marked the Union front just before and to the immediate right and left of the clump of trees there were more Confederates than Federals in action.

For the next few minutes this irregular rectangle of ground, a hundred yards deep by two or three hundred yards wide, was the bloody cockpit of the whole war, the place where men on foot with guns in their hands would arrive at a verdict. In this rectangle there was little work by the artillery. The Confederate guns to the west could not fire into this place without hitting their own men, and the Union guns here were out of action. A regular army battery of six guns commanded by Lieutenant Alonzo Cushing had been posted just north of the trees; by the time the Confederates came up to close range, five of the six guns had been put out of action, and when Cushing got off a final shot from the one gun that remained, he was killed and most of the gun crew went down with him. The climax of Pickett's charge was an infantry fight pure and simple.

RIGHT: The climax of the battle came on the afternoon of July 3, when some 15,000 men under general control of George Pickett struck Hancock's position on Cemetery Ridge after 140 Confederate guns had carried on an intensive bombardment. Aiming to strike the center of Hancock's line, with a "little clump of trees" as their landmark, the Confederates struck a position too strong to be carried with the numbers available, and their costly repulse ended the battle. Earlier, Ewell had unsuccessfully attacked Culp's Hill, while Union and Confederate cavalry fought a sharp but essentially meaningless engagement east of Gettysburg.

Afternoon of July 3

CHAMBERSBURG RD.

REMAINDER
OF HILL'S
III CORPS

EWELL'S
II
CORPS

YORK RD.

HAGERSTOWN RD.

Gettysburg

LEE

OHIO INFANTRY
FLANKING
THE CONFEDERATE
ATTACK

HOWARD'S
XI CORPS

PART OF NEWTON'S
I CORPS

CULP'S HILL

CEMETERY
HILL

SLOCUM'S
XII CORPS

MAIN COLUMN OF ASSAULT – PICKETT'S DIVISION
PLUS TWO DIVISIONS FROM HILL'S CORPS

HANCOCK'S II CORPS

GUNS SILENCED
BY THE
BOMBARDMENT

LITTLE CLUMP OF TREES

HIGH-
WATER MARK
OF THE ATTACK

FEDERAL ARTILLERY
THAT POUNDED
PICKETT'S MEN

BALTIMORE RD.

VERMONT INFANTRY
ATTACKING
PICKETT'S RIGHT FLANK

ELEMENTS FROM
NEWTON'S I CORPS
AND
SICKLES' III CORPS

MEADE

RANK OF LEE'S GUNS
WHOSE INTENSE
BOMBARDMENT
PAVED THE WAY FOR
PICKETT'S CHARGE

PEACH
ORCHARD

WHEAT
FIELD

SEDGWICK'S
VI CORPS
IN RESERVE

ROCK CREEK

EMMITSBURG RD.

TWO DIVISIONS
OF LONGSTREET'S
I CORPS

DEVIL'S
DEN

LITTLE
ROUND TOP

PLUM RUN

SYKES' V CORPS

TANEYTOWN RD.

ROUND TOP

N

One Mile

palacios

The artists have had a field day with Gettysburg for more than a century, and the most they can do is convey the impression of huge masses of men fighting furiously amid smoke and spurts of flame. Here are two conceptions of the supreme moments of Lee's attempt to break Meade's line on July 3. The degree of "realism" inherent in either picture is something for the individual viewer to determine for himself; the last of the men who might have borne personal, eyewitness testimony on the matter died long ago.

One on-the-spot artist visited the Union center on July 4 and sketched this grim picture of wrecked caissons and dead horses in one of the Federal battery positions.

It was fought out with unremitting fury. Some of Pickett's men broke in across the stone wall and knelt amid Cushing's idle guns to fire point-blank at the defending infantry. Some of the defenders found the fire too hot to bear and withdrew; on a narrow front, and for the moment, Pickett's men had actually broken the Union line. If they could widen the break and hold on to the ground gained until help came, they would have the battle won. . . .

Nowadays a visitor can stand by the clump of trees and see the whole battlefield, and it is hard to realize that hardly anything was visible to the men who were doing the fighting. This battle was fought in a blinding fog—a choking, reeking, impenetrable mist of powder smoke— smoke from the cannon and from the infantry rifles— lying close to the ground and drifting up toward the sky until some breeze might carry it away. Directly to the west of the focal point of the battle Lee himself watched and could see nothing—just an occasional glimpse of tossing flags and stabbing flames when the smoke would thin out temporarily. Longstreet ordered a brigade forward to reinforce Pickett, and the men could not see their objective because of the smoke clouds; they drifted far off to the right, came up against a waiting rank of Federal cannon and the spirited Vermonters, and were torn apart and compelled to retreat without having had the slightest effect on the course of the battle.

Several miles to the eastward Stuart's cavalry had at last gone into action, striking for the Union rear so that if the infantry assaults forced Meade to retreat, the Confederate horsemen could harry the fugitives and turn an orderly withdrawal into disordered rout. But the Federals were not retreating, and Union cavalry met Stuart's men, fought hard with charge and countercharge, and at last drove them away. Nothing could help Pickett's men. They would have to fight this one out on their own, there along the crest of Cemetery Ridge, with the broiling July sun shining down on the monstrous cloud blanket that piled thicker and thicker over the invisible scene of the fight.

For a brief time the Confederates had the advantage,

but they could not hold it. Crowding in to lay fire on the Federals in and on both sides of the fated little grove, they had an advantage in numbers, but there were too many Union soldiers in the immediate vicinity, and these were called over on the double. They came in swarms, formal military formation lost as they ran up to get into action at close range. The crowd became so dense that some of these reinforcements, halting to open fire on their enemies, hit their own comrades in front of them—just as some of the distant Confederate cannon, reaching out to hurt the Federals, struck down Confederates in the blind confusion. From the crest of Cemetery Ridge, perhaps a hundred yards behind the point of break-through, the Union regiments that had retreated formed ranks anew, regained their nerve, and opened a sharp counterattack. General Hancock, riding up to see that the front was restored, was shot from his horse with a wound that would keep him out of action until the following spring. General Gibbon also was shot down, severely wounded; but the Federal line stiffened and held without further direction, because in the end this was the private soldier's fight.

On the Confederate side it was Armistead who had led the contingent that broke the Federal line. He was still waving his sword, his black felt hat that had been on the point of the sword had slipped all the way down to the hilt; he laid his hand on one of dead Cushing's guns, urged his men on, a great figure of defiance—and then he fell with a mortal wound. An hour later, when Federal stretcher bearers were combing the littered field, he was still alive—enough so that he could stammer out a last message to his old friend Hancock. Then he died, while wounded Hancock was being carried from the field. The paths of these two men, which had parted in California more than two years earlier, had crossed again, for the last time.

Probably the most dramatic single moment at Gettysburg came when the Confederate Brigadier General Lewis Armistead, his slouch hat poised on his sword, led the heroic surge of men that broke into the Union line and overran one of Hancock's batteries near the clump of trees. Here is an artist's conception of the scene. Armistead got two or three hundred of his men through the line, but he himself was killed and most of those who followed him were shot down or taken prisoner.

ABOVE AND RIGHT: Cameras of the Civil War era were not capable of recording action shots, so no authentic photograph of men in combat in the battle of Gettysburg ever existed. The camera did make its record, however. These two scenes show a few of the many thousands killed at Gettysburg, waiting for the burial squads.

Then, suddenly, as the men from the North and the men from the South struggled in the dense battle smoke, the climax was passed. The Confederate wave had reached high-water mark and it began to ebb; watching from his post on the western ridge, Lee could see the human debris of a broken charge drifting back down the long slope. Military formations had been broken, but for the most part the men were going back sullenly, not panicky fugitives but soldiers ready to turn and fight if the Federals attempted a pursuit. The Federals made no attempt. They had beaten back the supreme effort Lee's army could make, but they had just about exhausted themselves doing it. They were content to see their enemies go away.

From his headquarters behind the lines Meade rode forward, saw the littered field, and learned that his soldiers had won a great victory. He took off his hat, apparently preparing to give a great shout, then thought better of it and said, reverently, "Thank God!" A mile away Lee rode forward to rally the men who had made the charge, telling them simply: "It is all my fault."

That night, after dark, Lee issued instructions for the organization of a wagon train to carry some of the thousands of wounded men back to Virginia. To an officer who received the orders, Lee said that he had never seen anything finer than the charge Pickett's men had made. If it had been supported properly, he said, it would have succeeded. Then his emotions broke through, and he cried aloud: "Oh, too bad! Too bad!"

Five

LONG REMEMBER

—♦—

With the repulse of Pickett's charge there was only one move Robert E. Lee could make. He had to get his army back to Virginia lest it be destroyed outright, as Abraham Lincoln hoped it might be. The bright possibilities that seemed to be open when general and army came north across the Potomac had vanished. What was left was the simple problem of survival.

Facing this problem, Lee did not panic; indeed, he seemed full of confidence. For the moment his offensive power was gone and he had to get away without delay, but he did not propose to be hurried about it and if the Yankees wanted one more fight here he would give it to them. On the night of July 3, while the shattered brigades that had gone storming up the slope of Cemetery Ridge were getting themselves sorted out, Lee ordered a contraction of his lines. Ewell's men were pulled back from the north and east of Cemetery Hill, and Longstreet's troops were disengaged from the tangled thickets and fields in front of the Round Tops; the wagons containing such wounded men as could be moved were started west, heading for the gaps in South Mountain before swinging south for the river crossings; and on July 4 most of the army stood its ground, warily eyeing the Federals on the high ground to the east. The Confederates more than half expected Meade to attack them and more than half

General Robert E. Lee, looking as always a little larger than life-size . . . the knight "sans peur et sans reproche." (The Bettmann Archive, Inc.)

hoped he would try it; they had failed in their own attack, and the failure had left the army half crippled, but the men had not a doubt in the world that they could smash any offensive the Union soldiers might make. If such an attack were made and beaten back, the whole Gettysburg venture would look a good deal less like the Confederate disaster which in fact it was.

General Meade had no intention of making such an attack. His army had fought and won the most prodigious battle of the war, and if the victory had been purely defensive it had nevertheless been decisive. Meade would not risk diminishing the victory by making what looked to him like an unnecessary attack. Lee had to retreat anyway, his entire invasion scheme in collapse, but if his army had been beaten, it was still as dangerous as a wounded panther. Meade would follow it closely, and if a good chance presented itself he would strike, but he would be very cautious. For the moment he would be happy enough to see the Confederate army leave Northern soil.

Most of Meade's men agreed with him, and the Confederates later asserted that they would have had everything to gain and nothing to lose if Meade had gone over to the offensive immediately after Gettysburg. Indeed, the one man who was seriously displeased by Meade's decision was Abraham Lincoln, President of the United States and, under the Constitution, commander in chief of the nation's armed forces. Lincoln from the beginning had seen what the professional soldiers had mostly failed to see—that when Lee cut his ties with Virginia and marched deep into Northern territory he risked losing his whole army. In the North he could be cut off and compelled to destroy himself in a vain fight to escape. The victory at Gettysburg had been notable, but it was only half of the story as Lincoln saw it. One way or another, Lee's army should be kept from ever going south across the Potomac. To rejoice that he had been driven away from "our soil," as so many Northern patriots were doing, was beside the point, and Lincoln angrily asked his private secretary, John Hay: "Will our generals never get that idea out of their heads? The whole country is our soil." . . . The union was endangered, as Lincoln saw it, not because Lee's army was north of the Potomac but because Lee's army existed at all.

Lee got his army down to the Potomac crossings at last, followed by Meade's army but not actively pursued, and because the river was swollen past fording and Lee

RIGHT: Retreating from Gettysburg, Lee sent his wagon train (including the wagons loaded with wounded men) round-about by Chambersburg, and with the bulk of his army cut cross-country to Hagerstown and over to the Potomac cross-ing at Williamsport. Meade followed on a long arc that led down through Frederick, cutting west via Middletown to come up against Lee's temporary lines at Williamsport. Lee was delayed here because of high water in the Potomac, but he built an impromptu bridge and on July 13 got his army safely across. Meade had ordered an assault for the next day, but when his troops moved forward the Confederate lines were empty. Lee's army had escaped. The momentous Gettysburg campaign had passed into history.

Lee's Retreat

0   Miles   20

had no pontoon train, the Confederates had to wait for a few days, in and around Williamsport. Meade assembled his troops facing Lee, found at a council of war that his generals did not think an attack advisable, made up his mind at last to make such an attack anyway — and on the morning of July 14, when his infantry moved forward to make its fight, learned that Lee had gone across the river during the night, leaving nothing but a rear guard to impede the Yankee advance. The great Gettysburg campaign was over. If, as Lincoln believed, Lee had been in danger of losing his army then and there, he had at last escaped. But in any case this chapter of the war was finished. The invasion of the North had failed, once and for all.

It is easier to see it now than it was at the time, but in fact the great turning point of the war had been reached and passed. Gettysburg drew a good part of its significance from something that happened simultaneously a thousand miles to the southwest. At Vicksburg, Mississippi, on July 4, while the armies in Pennsylvania stared at each other across fields reeking with the dreadful presence of thousands of unburied bodies, General John Pem-

berton surrendered 30,000 Confederate soldiers, the
great stronghold at Vicksburg, and control of the Mississippi Valley to General U. S. Grant. In Lincoln's memorable phrase, the Father of Waters now rolled unvexed to
the sea. The Southern Confederacy had been cut in half.
Now it could not hope to muster the strength to over-
throw the Federal government.

Lee had just time enough, after the defeat at Gettysburg,
to get his army safely south of the Potomac; when Meade
assaulted his lines, at Falling Waters near Williamsport,
Maryland, on July 13, all but a Confederate rear guard had
got back into Virginia. Here the artist depicts an assault on
part of the rear guard by a Federal cavalry regiment.

For some thousands of dejected Confederates, the road away from Gettysburg led to a Northern prison camp. Here an artist shows a column of prisoners starting the long march to captivity after the repulse of Pickett's charge on the afternoon of July 3.

This gave Gettysburg added significance. As Lincoln privately complained, Lee had escaped when he might have been destroyed, but Gettysburg nevertheless had been a prodigious Federal achievement. Here the Confederacy had made its supreme bid to win its independence by a decisive triumph north of the Potomac. It had failed—when all was said and done—had failed because it simply was not strong enough. It could not knock the North out of the war or win the overwhelming advantage that would bring recognition by the British. It might yet win the war, to be sure, by hanging on in a grim defensive until the Northern people and their government concluded that victory was not going to be worth what it would cost; but outright victory, forcing the kind of decision the government at Richmond wanted, just was not in the cards. Not after Gettysburg; not after Gettysburg interpreted in the light of Vicksburg.

For the defeat at Gettysburg exposed a fundamental flaw in Confederate strategy. At least one reason for the invasion of the North had been the hope that pressure here would compel the government at Washington to withdraw support from Grant, thereby enabling the South to save Vicksburg and the Mississippi Valley. This had not happened. Once Grant got Pemberton and his army locked up in Vicksburg, Washington sent him strong reinforcements, in men and in matériel. He lacked for nothing he needed to bring Pemberton to surrender, and Lee's march into Pennsylvania did not cause the Lincoln administration to turn a hair. Not one man, gun, or wagon-load of supplies was withheld from Grant because of the invasion of Pennsylvania. Even if Lee had actually driven the Army of the Potomac away from the Gettysburg heights, the Union would still have taken Vicksburg. This gamble was lost before it was made.

In addition, the Gettysburg campaign had involved the Army of Northern Virginia in the kind of fight that it had very little chance to win. Gettysburg had been one of the costliest of battles. In the three days of fighting the Confederates had lost more than 20,000 men—slightly less than a third of Lee's combat strength. Federal losses, to be sure, were higher—at 23,000; but Federal strength was greater, too, and in proportion to the numbers available the Confederate loss was heavier than the Union loss.

A year later, when the Army of the Potomac was slowly and painfully fighting its way south across war-ravaged Virginia, it was argued that the Union was engaged in a simple war of attrition, accepting heavy losses for the sake of inflicting heavy losses, knowing that Northern resources were far greater than Southern resources. As a matter of fact, the war of attrition had begun much earlier . . . in the Gettysburg campaign. When the South undertook to invade the North in the face of Northern superiority in man power, it made a war of attrition inevitable. Not even Robert E. Lee could win that kind of fight.

The shortcomings of Lee's subordinates at Gettysburg fall into better focus once this fact is appreciated. Ewell might indeed have been dilatory (where his predecessor, Stonewall Jackson, would have moved like jagged lightning) in mounting the attack on Cemetery Hill and Culp's Hill late in the afternoon of the first day; Stuart may have left Lee blind by going far afield and getting his cavalry corps blocked out of the play at the crucial moment of invasion; Longstreet may have been slow, handling his part of the fighting on the second and third days without the furious driving energy Lee wanted—all the complaints on these points, made not by Lee himself but by his admirers, may have been justified. But the hard fact remains that when an army like Lee's took the offensive against a larger army, in the enemy's own country, it committed itself to the wrong kind of fight. At Gettysburg it could do nothing but get in close and slug until something broke. What broke was its own offensive power.

In addition to all other considerations, there is a final point: Lee at Gettysburg was fighting against a man who never wore a uniform or fought a battle: the eminent Illinois civilian Abraham Lincoln. The whole rationale of the Confederate offensive that summer (aside from the purely minor matter of temporarily relieving Virginia of the weight of the war and collecting supplies in Pennsylvania) was the belief that the Northern government would crack under the strain—that it would take troops away from General Grant, lose confidence in final victory when it saw Confederate troops in the Northern heartland, find the price of the war too great to pay, and so consent at last to a formal separation.

None of this happened. The Northern government did not collapse, did not waver in its resolve to go on with the war until slavery and secession were both dead, did not flinch at the fearful price that would still have to be paid . . . and for "the Northern government," read "Abraham Lincoln." He was Lee's ultimate opponent at Gettysburg; he won, partly because Meade and the Army of the Potomac stood firm, but even more because Lincoln himself was where Lee's army could not reach him.

In the fall of 1863, after the armies had gone their ways and entered upon new campaigns, Lincoln himself went to Gettysburg to talk about what had been done there: what had been done, and what it all might possibly mean.

The dead men were all under the ground by now and on the low hill and the long ridge there was the beginning of a great park. There was a formal cemetery, with the soldiers' graves arranged in neat arcs of a series of concentric circles, headstones flush with the ground bearing names and unit identifications . . . hundreds of headstones bearing no names but simply testifying to the presence of bodies that would go forever unidentified. The little clump of trees still stood at the summit of the long slope that came up from the Emmitsburg road, and although it is so small that a couple of good woodsmen could have felled all its trees in one morning, it is nevertheless the most famous little grove in all America. And thousands of Lincoln's fellow countrymen went to Gettysburg for the dedication of the cemetery, and heard famous orator Edward Everett deliver a polished address that left no echoes whatever, and at last stood in silence while Lincoln spoke the few sentences that made cemetery and park something more than a simple memorial to human courage.

No one could explain it better than Abraham Lincoln. When he said that people would never forget what the soldiers had done on this battlefield, he added that no one would long remember what anyone said there; and this was a slight mistake, because what he said there is something the American people will always turn to when they want to know why this great hour of tragedy had to take place and what it meant in the growth of a great nation.

Two or three generations earlier, Lincoln reminded

his listeners, the American people had brought forth a nation "conceived in liberty and dedicated to the proposition that all men are created equal." The terrible Civil War itself, he said, was simply a matter of testing whether that nation and the dream that inspired it could go on living. The unlimited potential embodied in the great word "America" depended on the way the challenge was met. The soldiers had done their part . . . to the last full measure of their devotion. The rest, then and thereafter, would be up to the living.

To the living of all subsequent generations, including this one, Gettysburg left an unending responsibility. A nation built on the idea that all men—*all men*—are of equal worth and equal rights summons every one of its citizens to a life-long commitment to put that idea into practical effect.

Gettysburg, then, was the price we paid for our service under that great concept. It was one step in a long progression; not an end, but a beginning—a pledge written in blood that freedom should be reborn in every generation.

So Lincoln explained it, looking across the graves to the truth that gave them meaning. That is why Americans will long remember what was done and what was said on this greatest of their battlefields.

INDEX

NOTE: all illustrations are designated by *italicized* numbers

Rodes, Major General Robert,
25, 32
Round Tops, 31, 46, 50–51, 54, 58,
63, 73, 97

Secretary of War, Confederate, 5
Sedgwick, Major General John, 39
Seminary Ridge, 26, 29, 37, 71
Sharpsburg (Antietam), 7, 35
Sickles, Major General Dan, 19,
39, 42, 54, 58, 63
Signal Corps participation, 43
Slocum, Major General Henry W.,
39, 47, 72, 76
South Carolina, war strategy in, 6
South Mountain, 71, 98
Stanton, Edwin M., Secretary of
War under President Lincoln,
17
Stuart, Major General James Ewell
Brown ("Jeb"), 13–14, 37, 72,
91, 106
Sykes, Major General George, 39,
43, 46, 58, 70

Tennessee, Confederate Army
near, 6
Trees", "little clump of, on Cemetery Ridge, 81, 83, 85, 86,
90–91, 93, 108

Union Army. See Federal Army
Union artillerists withdrawing a
gun by hand, 55
Union defender, a, 62
Union defense, General Hancock
directing, 80

Union defenses on Little Round
Top, 44, 45
Union soldiers at Culp's Hill, brief
respite for, 66, 66

Vermont infantry, 82, 91
Vicksburg, Mississippi: Confederate fortress of, 5, 6; siege of, 9;
surrender of General Pemberton's soldiers to General Grant
at, 102–3, 105
Vincent, Colonel Strong, 70
Virginia, war strategy in, 4, 5, 6,
7–8, 13, 14, 105–6. See also
Blue Ridge Mountains; Chancellorsville, battle of; Richmond, drive on; Winchester

Wadsworth, Brigadier General
James, 21
Wagon train and wounded men of
Lee, retreating from Gettys-
burg, 100
Waiting for the burial squads, 94, 95
War of attrition, 106
Warren, Major General G. K., 43,
46, 71
Washington, D.C.: war strategy
to defend, 10, 12, 18; support
of General Grant by, 105,
107. See also Bull Run, second
battle of
Williamsport, Maryland, Lee's
retreat through, 100, 102
Winchester, Ewell's victory at, 11

York, Pennsylvania, 12, 14, 25

These pu

Sadie loves training her new poodle puppy, Truffle, to do tricks. Truffle is so good that a classmate talks Sadie into entering the school talent show.

As the night of the show gets closer, however, Sadie gets a bad case of stage fright. She's not sure she can perform in front of her whole school! Will her big night be ruined?

More magical tales!

Puppy Powers
A Wishbone Come True
KRISTIN EARHART

Puppy Powers
Wag, You're It!
KRISTIN EARHART

Puppy Powers
Hide and Go Fetch
KRISTIN EARHART

■SCHOLASTIC
www.scholastic.com

Cover art by Vivienne To
Cover design by Jeannine Riske

APPEALS TO
2ND-3RD GRADERS

READING LEVEL
GRADE 3

More leveling information for this book:
www.scholastic.com/readinglevel

Take a Bow-Wow

Get your paws on all of the Puppy Powers books!

#1: A Wishbone Come True

#2: Wag, You're It!

Puppy Powers

Take a Bow-Wow

BY KRISTIN EARHART
ILLUSTRATED BY VIVIENNE TO

Scholastic Inc.

ISBN 978-0-545-61761-1

Text copyright © 2014 by Kristin Earhart
Cover and interior art copyright © 2014 by Scholastic Inc.

12 11 10 9 8 7 6 5 4 3 2 1   14 15 16 17 18 19/0
Printed in the U.S.A.   40
First printing, August 2014

To Maggie, Kali, and Blue.
Thanks for the memories.

⭐ Chapter 1 ⭐

"I can't believe you went through with it," Henry said, shaking his head.

"I know," Sadie agreed, her eyes wide. "I can't believe I did either." She put a wad of newspaper in Henry's hands. It had his name on it. Next, she pulled another clump of newspaper off the same shelf. This one was marked *Sadie Reynolds*.

"Well, I totally believe it," said their friend Lexi. She cradled her clump of newspaper in her arms. The three friends

headed to a table at the far end of the art room. "I'm proud of you, Sadie."

"I just hope it will be worth it," Sadie admitted. She placed her damp newspaper bundle in front of her. Then, in one easy motion, she pulled her long, black curly hair into a ponytail and snapped a rubber band around it. Next, she tugged the wet paper away from her clay sculpture, piece by piece. It didn't look at all like a dog. It looked like a wet rock. She had a lot of work to do.

"It'll totally be worth it," Lexi said. She gave Sadie a reassuring smile.

Sadie was glad that they could talk in art class. She had been looking forward to telling her friends about her plan all morning, but there hadn't been time before school.

"I just wish you had told us you were in a piano recital. We would have come to cheer you on," Lexi added.

"Um, Sadie doesn't like to perform in front of people," Henry reminded Lexi. "That's the whole point."

Henry was right. Sadie hated getting up in front of people. Lexi didn't really get that. Lexi liked the attention. Sadie was glad that Henry understood.

"I only did it because of my parents' promise. They better not change their minds." Sadie crossed her fingers and then gave them a kiss for extra luck. She needed it.

"You performed in a piano recital. In front of real people," Lexi said. "They'll keep their promise."

Sadie was pretty sure she could count on her parents. They were good like that. Still, everything had to work exactly as she had planned or it could be months before she'd get another chance.

"Mr. Power got the poodles in at the beginning of the week," she explained.

"He says he doesn't get poodles that often. I really love one of them, and I just hope he's still there when my parents come by tomorrow. They have to leave work early and everything."

Lexi and Henry nodded. They both knew Mr. Power. He was the owner of Castleton's very own pet center, Power's Pets. Lexi, Henry, and Sadie all helped Mr. Power in the store. Their friend Max, who was in another class, volunteered with them, too. Sometimes they had to

clean out the guinea pig cages (yuck), but usually they got to play with the kittens or feed the turtles. Just last week, Henry had spent his whole volunteer time teaching the store parrot, Mango, fun new phrases.

"Why do you want to get a poodle?" Henry asked. "Is it because you like their poofy, frilly haircuts?"

Sadie sighed. Why did people always think that poodles were fancy-pants dogs? It wasn't true at all. Sadie knew that poodles were actually great athletes. "For your information," Sadie began, "the classic poodle haircut dates back to when poodles were famous water dogs. Owners cut their poodles' hair so that it wasn't too heavy for swimming. Poodles were great retrievers for hunting ducks and stuff," Sadie explained. She had read a lot about dogs. Recently, she'd started reading anything she could find about poodles.

"I never knew that," Henry admitted. "It's interesting, but it doesn't explain why you want a poodle."

"It isn't that I *want* a poodle," she replied. "It's that I *need* a poodle. My dad has bad allergies. If he's around dogs, his eyes get all red and his nose gets all stuffy." Sadie had seen it happen a bunch of times. It wasn't pretty. "But the good news is that poodles don't bug him at all. Poodles are practically hypoallergenic. That means they don't make people sneeze as much. Mr. Power told me."

He had mentioned it to her parents, too. Because of her dad's allergies, Sadie had thought a dog was out of the question. Poodles gave her hope! But even after talking to the kind, old owner of the pet store, her parents still weren't convinced. That's when Sadie had come up with her plan.

Her parents had really wanted her to play in the piano recital. Sadie had been

taking lessons for three years, but she had always refused to be part of her teacher's recitals. This year, Sadie agreed to perform — if she could get a dog.

It was a brilliant idea, and her parents had agreed. Sadie couldn't believe it.

Still, Sadie had to get through the recital. She hated feeling unprepared, so she practiced a lot. The only way she could get over her stage fright was to practice, practice, practice. She played her piece until she knew it by heart.

The recital had been just last weekend. It had gone well. Sadie had survived! Her parents had been proud. Then, that very night, Mr. Power had called to say that he was expecting a small litter of poodle pups that week. It was almost like magic.

Sadie had stopped by after school on Wednesday with her sitter. Sure enough, there were five poodles in the puppy pen: two silver puppies, two white puppies, and

one cream pup. They were all adorable, but there was something about the little cream-colored puppy that had caught Sadie's attention. She wasn't sure what that something was, but she was sure that he was the only puppy for her.

"I hope it works out," Lexi said with a burst of excitement. "I'm so happy for you!" Her face was all smiles, and she clapped her hands at least ten times.

"Why are you so happy, Lexi?" Isa Graham asked from the next table.

"Well, it's Sadie's news," Lexi began. She looked over to Sadie, but Sadie just looked down at her clay blob.

Henry answered for her. "Sadie's going to get a puppy. A poodle, because her dad's allergic to other dogs."

"Oh, I love poodles," Isa exclaimed, pushing a strand of chestnut-colored hair over her shoulder. "You're so lucky, Sadie. My parents have been promising me a

puppy for ages, but I got my ears pierced instead."

Sadie nodded, noticing a big blue earring sparkling through Isa's long locks. It felt weird, hearing Isa say she was "lucky." To Sadie, Isa Graham seemed like a girl who was swimming in luck and good fortune. Isa always seemed to have the coolest clothes and the most exciting stories. Sadie had kind of assumed that Isa already had a dog, or two or three.

"Where are you getting your poodle, Sadie?" Isa asked.

Sadie hesitated. She had really wanted the puppy to be more of a secret, especially since it wasn't a sure thing. "From Power's Pets," she answered, twisting a strand of loose hair.

"Oh, that's the new pet store on the square," responded Isa. "I'll have to check it out. Maybe my dad can take me today or tomorrow!"

Sadie just nodded. She had a feeling that when Isa Graham went to a pet store, she got to leave with a new pet. And Sadie had a bad feeling that she knew which pet Isa Graham would pick. That would be just Sadie's luck.

✫ Chapter 2 ✫

The next day, Sadie, Lexi, and Henry met their friend Max just outside Power's Pets. They were all certain that Sadie was going to adopt her puppy that afternoon. That is, everyone was sure except Sadie.

Power's Pets had only been open a few months. In that short time, Lexi and Max had both adopted puppies of their own. Lexi had a frisky black-and-brown pup with floppy ears. Max's puppy was a fluffy golden retriever with a jolly grin.

All day at school, Sadie had kept her fingers crossed for luck. She double-checked now to make sure they were still intertwined. She walked into the pet-center door behind her friends. "Hi, Mr. Power! We're here!" the group called out.

"Happy Friday," a voice replied. "I'll be right there!"

Sadie had been waiting for this moment all day. But instead of going straight to the puppy pen, she stalled in the middle of the store. She didn't want to know if the cream-colored puppy was gone.

"Don't worry," Henry said. "He's still here."

"He is?" Sadie asked, rushing over to the play area. "He is!" she exclaimed when she saw his sweet black eyes and coat of shaggy curls.

"He's supercute," Max said.

"I know," Sadie agreed. She looked up at the clock. It wasn't even 4:00 yet. She wondered when her parents would get there.

"Hello, hello!" Mr. Power said, coming over. "We have a busy day today. I wrote out a list of things we need to do."

He handed the list to Henry, and the three others crowded around him. "I want to feed Mango!" Henry said.

"I'll help Mr. Power clip the kittens' claws," Max offered.

"Good, that leaves feeding the lizards and the fish for us," Lexi said to Sadie.

A short time later, Lexi and Sadie were staring into the fish tanks. The electric-blue and cherry-red fish were swimming in figure eights.

"I'm so relieved that Isa didn't come in and take the cream-colored puppy yesterday," Sadie said.

"Why were you so worried?" Lexi asked.

Sadie shrugged. "I don't know."

"You can't let Isa get to you, Sadie," Lexi said. "You need to stand up for yourself. When you talk to me, Henry, or Max, you say just what you're thinking. But you're different with other kids."

Sadie didn't know what to say. She knew Lexi was right, but she couldn't explain it. "I just feel good around you guys. It's easy to be myself."

"You should be yourself around everyone," Lexi said.

Sadie sighed. "It's not that easy." She wasn't sure she could make Lexi understand. Lexi never got tongue-tied or ended up saying way too much. Sometimes Sadie started talking and she couldn't stop. The rest of the time, she couldn't find the words at all, so she didn't say anything, even when she wanted to. All or nothing: Sadie didn't know which was worse.

"Hey, Mr. Power and I are done with the kittens' claws," Max said. He had

walked over to Lexi and Sadie. Henry had come over, too.

Sadie half smiled. Now that they were there, it would be the end of her talk with Lexi. Sadie was relieved.

She watched Mr. Power turn away from the kittens and head their way.

"We're expecting your parents soon. Aren't we, Sadie?" He glanced at his old pocket watch. He raised his eyebrows, clicked the watch closed, and slipped it back in his vest. "Well, we don't have too much time before they'll be here. If you know the puppy that you'd like, we can get started."

Sadie bit her lip. She was too excited to speak!

"Max mentioned that you have a favorite," the store owner said in a helpful tone. "Who's the lucky pup?"

Sadie took a deep breath and exhaled. She could feel her smile pushing her cheeks

up into her eyes. She could not remember ever feeling so happy. "The little cream-colored one," she said finally.

"That is a pup that knows what he wants," Mr. Power said. "He's got a mind of his own."

Sadie frowned. "What do you mean?"

"Oh, just that he doesn't follow the other puppies around. He does what he wants to do," Mr. Power explained. He bent down and reached into the puppy pen. "Would you like to hold him?"

"Yes, please," replied Sadie as she took the poodle in her arms. Her fingers were immediately lost under the puppy's lush curls. They felt so silky and smooth. The puppy was amazingly calm. He looked her right in the eye.

Sadie stared back. She couldn't look away. All at once, she felt something bump into her side. Then she felt it again.

"Look at his tail!" Henry cried.

"Wow. I've never seen a tail wag so hard," Max added.

"I think he likes you," Lexi said.

"Yes, I'm sure he does." Mr. Power smiled. "I guess it's time to tell you about his trick. Did Max and Lexi tell you about their puppies' tricks?"

Sadie shook her head.

"Well, I'm sure they'll agree that a puppy's trick is very important." Mr. Power

took the poodle into his own arms as he spoke. "You have to ask them to do it in just the right way." He set the puppy on the floor.

Sadie wasn't all that interested in tricks. She just wanted a new friend — a fuzzy, funny, frisky new friend — but she listened politely.

"This puppy can chase his tail extra fast. It's pretty cute," Mr. Power explained with a laugh. "To ask him to perform the trick, you clap once and say, 'Bet you can't catch it.'"

Sadie grinned. It seemed like such a funny thing to say!

"How about you give it a try?" the store owner suggested. "When you want him to stop, just say, 'Stop.'"

Sadie nodded and knelt down without saying a word. The puppy gazed at her with his sweet, serious eyes. He seemed to be waiting.

At that exact moment, the door opened and Isa Graham strode into the pet store with her father.

Sadie felt her heart jump into her throat. Then it fell to the bottom of her belly, and it stayed right there.

✮ Chapter 3 ✮

"Hi," Isa said to the group. "This is my dad. Oh, Dad, look at that adorable puppy. Isn't he the cutest?" Isa rushed over and knelt down to pet him.

Sadie was stunned. She looked at Isa. She wanted the other girl to know that she could not have this puppy.

Sadie imagined what would happen next. Isa would tell her dad that she wanted the cream-colored puppy. Then Isa would get to take the puppy home.

Sadie wanted to say something, but she couldn't seem to move her tongue.

As Isa rubbed the puppy's ears, she leaned forward and touched her nose to his. She didn't seem to realize everyone was watching her.

The puppy looked from Sadie to Isa, and back again. Gazing at Sadie, he barked and wagged his tail. He took a step toward her and barked two more times. Then, with an immediate burst of energy, the puppy started to scamper in circles, right at Sadie's feet. He bolted around and around, growling playfully. He was chasing his tail, just like Mr. Power had said. The puppy was doing his special trick all by himself.

As Sadie watched in awe, silver stars seemed to swirl around the puppy. Stars whirled around her, too. Suddenly, Sadie didn't feel nervous.

"Hi, Isa," Sadie said. "This is my new puppy. As soon as my mom and dad come, I'm going to take him home." She smiled and took another deep breath.

"Stop," she said to the puppy. The little dog skidded to a halt. His pink tongue drooped from his mouth. He lay down, panting. The silver sparkles had disappeared, but the puppy had not lost his adorable glow. He was just the cutest puppy Sadie could imagine.

For a moment, it was like it was just Sadie and the puppy in the store. She wrapped her fingers behind his ears and gave him a super scratch. "You're such a good boy, aren't you? You almost caught your tail that time, didn't you?" The puppy rubbed his chilly, wet nose all over her hands and wrists.

"Well, I just wanted to come see all the animals," said Isa. She reached out and grabbed her father's hand. "Thanks for bringing me, Dad. I really like this place. Maybe someday I could get a puppy from here, too?"

"Maybe," her dad replied, smoothing the long hair on Isa's back. He smiled at Mr. Power and the group of kids before heading out the door.

Lexi quickly came over and sat down on the tile floor next to Sadie. With her heels tucked beneath her, she put her hands on her knees and leaned close to

Sadie's ear. "That was awesome, Sadie," she said.

Sadie raked her bottom teeth over her upper lip and searched her friend's face. She wondered what would have happened if she had not said anything. Would Isa have asked her dad for the puppy? Sadie didn't know.

"So, you got to see this pup's trick," Mr. Power said, walking over. "Pretty cute, huh?"

"Definitely," Sadie replied, stroking the puppy along the back. "I didn't even have to ask him. He just did it on his own."

The old man rubbed his whiskers and seemed to investigate the puppy, looking at him front to back.

It made Sadie nervous, seeing the store owner examine the puppy so closely. Worry started to well up inside her. She looped a loose curl around her finger until she couldn't stand it any longer. "You

know, you never told me what this puppy's name is," she blurted. "I mean, it doesn't really matter because I would love him even if he's named Cauliflower Surprise, but I kind of want to know so I know what I should call him. I can't keep calling him 'This Puppy.'" She swallowed quickly, before more words tumbled out.

Mr. Power didn't answer right away. He bent down and put a gentle hand under the puppy's chin. He leaned close to the puppy, just as Lexi had to Sadie. He lifted the pup's soft, floppy ear and whispered.

When he was done, he looked at Sadie. He seemed to have a twinkle in his eye. "This puppy doesn't have a name yet. I guess that will be up to you. Will you call him Cauliflower Surprise?"

Sadie smiled and rolled her eyes, but not in a mean way. "No, I think I'll call him Truffle," she answered. "A long time ago, people used poodles to sniff out truffles in the ground. They were good working dogs. Today, people use pigs more than poodles. But I like the name Truffle anyway."

"What's a truffle?" Max asked.

"It's a fungus that is a lot like a mushroom, but fancier," Sadie explained.

Henry made a face. "I think I'd call him Cauliflower Surprise instead."

"No, I'm sticking with Truffle," Sadie insisted. When he heard his name, the puppy looked up at Sadie with kind, bright eyes. Sadie was confident that the name was perfect, just like her puppy.

⭐ Chapter 4 ⭐

Life with a puppy was everything Sadie had imagined: fun, fun, and more fun! In some ways, he was too much fun. Truffle wanted to play as soon as Sadie woke up. He wanted to play while she ate breakfast, and he wanted to play when she was getting ready for bed. Sadie wanted to play with him all of the time, too.

"Remember our agreement," Sadie's mom said across the table. It was a school day. Sadie was throwing Truffle a ball in

between taking bites of cereal. "Your puppy cannot interfere with your other responsibilities," her mom reminded her.

Truffle bounded away and tracked down the ball in seconds. "He's not interfering," Sadie insisted as Truffle trotted back with the rubber ball in his mouth. Her mom sounded serious, but Sadie wasn't worried. Her mom loved Truffle. He kept her mom company in the kitchen, lifting his nose and smelling all of the wonderful aromas of her cooking. Sadie's dad was just waiting for Truffle to be big enough to go jogging with him. Truffle was already a member of the family.

Still, her mom had a point. Truffle did demand a lot of her attention. It was hard enough for Sadie to get her homework done with the puppy staring at her, but practicing piano was even worse! He would bark and prance around. He seemed

to spin in time with the music and wouldn't stop until Sadie paused and gave him a good pet.

It was several days before Sadie thought about Truffle's special trick again. She and Truffle had walked to the local dog park with her dad.

"It's good that we're getting this puppy outside before it rains," Mr. Reynolds said to Sadie. "He needs to get rid of some of his energy. He's way too hyper when he's cooped up." Then he looked at Truffle and smiled. "You don't like being stuck inside, do you? You like to run and play and show off."

RRRufff!

When Truffle heard Mr. Reynolds talk like that, his ears perked up. He jumped on his hind feet and tugged on the leash.

"Dad, you're getting him all excited," Sadie said.

"That's fine," her dad replied. "That's why we're going to the park. Isn't it, boy?" Sadie liked to see this side of her dad. Truffle made him a little silly, like a kid.

Once they arrived, Sadie took the leash off and let the puppy run around. She had a rubber ball that looked like a globe. She threw it, and Truffle raced after it, running at full speed. He liked to catch it in the air, or spin around after he scooped it off the ground. Lots of people pointed at him and complimented Sadie on her cute

dog. The owner of another poodle started talking to her dad.

"Hey, Sadie!" a voice called from the other side of the park.

Sadie looked up. She was surprised to see Isa Graham waving at her. The girl hurried across the park, skirting around leashes and chew toys in her shiny purple boots. She held a clipboard tight against her chest. Sadie bit her upper lip.

"Hey," Isa said again when she was just steps away. "Did you bring your new puppy?"

Sadie nodded.

"Where is he?" Isa asked.

"Over there." Sadie pointed. Truffle was rolling around with a much bigger dog, nipping at his paws.

"He's so cute," Isa said under her breath. She raised her clipboard and tapped a pink pen against the paper.

Sadie could tell Isa had something on her mind.

"Sadie," Isa began in a serious tone, "I'm here at the dog park raising money to help save the wolves. I'm on the school talent show committee — we're selling tickets to support wildlife organizations."

"Really?" Sadie asked. She was listening to Isa, but she was watching Truffle.

"Right now, wolves are struggling," Isa continued. "They are losing places to live in the wild. I guess that as a dog lover, you care about wolves."

Sadie nodded.

"Would you like to volunteer?" Isa asked. "You could be in the talent show."

Sadie started to nod again, but quickly stopped. "Oh, no. I can't do that," she answered.

"Please, Sadie?"

Sadie did care about the wolves. She

had read all about them. Scientists had proven that today's dogs are related to wolves. Also, Sadie knew that wolves played an important part in the balance of nature. She wanted to help, but there was no way she was going to be in a talent show. She had already performed at the piano recital and that had been bad enough.

Luckily, Truffle came running back to her, and both girls forgot about the talent show while they played with him. Truffle wanted to tug on a stick, and Isa put down her clipboard so she could pull with both hands.

After a while, Isa said she should go. "I need to find some more people or we won't have a talent show at all." Hearing this, Sadie felt kind of bad. As Isa started to turn away, Truffle barked at Sadie. He barked and wagged his tail, sticking his curly rump in the air. He stared at Sadie

the way he had at the pet center. Sadie
remembered that it had been just before he
did his trick.

"Do you want to do your special trick?"
she asked.

RRRufff.

"He's going to do his trick?" Isa asked.
"I've got to stay to see that."

"Okay," Sadie said, pulling a treat out
of her pocket. She clapped and said, "Bet
you can't catch it."

Truffle took off in a tight circle, chasing after his short, cottony tail. Both Sadie and Isa laughed. Suddenly, Sadie noticed silver stars swirling in the air, just like at Power's Pets. She watched as the stars shimmered and danced. Then she looked down at Truffle and said, "Stop." She bent over to give the puppy his treat.

Sadie thought about her piano recital. She had sounded pretty good. And afterward, she'd felt proud. Maybe performing one more time wouldn't be so bad. "You know, Isa, I can help. I can be in the talent show."

Isa was writing on her clipboard. "I knew I could count on you, Sadie!" she exclaimed. "Thank you so much. You'll be great. Do you know what your talent will be?" Isa asked. She held her pen at the ready.

Sadie swallowed. "Um, piano?" She said it like a question, but there was really

no question about it. Playing the piano was the only talent she had.

"Great," Isa replied. "You'll be just great." With that, Isa patted Sadie on the back and headed across the lawn. She turned around when she was several strides away and yelled, "Thanks so much, Sadie!"

Sadie could hardly believe her ears. She barely remembered agreeing to be in the talent show. What was she thinking? Truffle rubbed up against her leg and gave a happy yip.

"Thrilled," Mrs. Reynolds said into the phone. "We're just thrilled that Sadie volunteered to be part of the talent show." She paused and smiled over at her daughter. "Of course you should come. You're her grandmother! Maybe Monica wants to come, too."

Sadie spun her finger around one of her tight curls. She sighed. "Come on, Truffle," she said finally, heading to her room. "Henry and Lexi will be here soon."

Sadie read a book on her beanbag chair

and Truffle played with a chew toy until the doorbell rang. When Sadie answered the door, she was relieved to see her friends. "Hey, let's go to the backyard. Truffle needs some exercise."

Lexi and Henry shrugged and then followed her. They waved to Sadie's mom. Mrs. Reynolds seemed to be on the phone with someone new, but she was still talking about the upcoming talent show.

"Sadie, it's really great that you got over your stage fright, or whatever it was," Lexi

said. "Isa is super happy that you're doing the talent show."

"That's just it. I'm *not* over my stage fright," Sadie admitted. She threw a Frisbee, and Truffle took off, chasing it. "I do not want to perform at all."

"Then why did you volunteer?" Henry asked.

"I don't know," Sadie answered.

"Wait. Did Isa force you to say yes?" Lexi asked.

"No," said Sadie. She did have a hard time saying no to Isa, but the other girl did not *make* her say yes. "At least I don't think so. It was weird. For like a minute, I was just sure I should do it." She let out a long breath. "Then, just like that, I wished I hadn't."

Truffle came back, and Sadie threw the Frisbee again.

"That is weird," Lexi agreed. "So what are you going to do?"

"My mom is so happy. I don't know how I'm going to back out," Sadie said, "but I have to. I can't play piano in front of all those people. I'll just freeze up."

"How did you get through the recital?" Henry asked.

"I practiced like crazy," she answered.

"Well, just do that again," Lexi suggested with a shrug. "It can't be that bad. Maybe it will be easier this time."

Sadie hoped that was true. At least at the recital, she knew she would get a puppy after she was done. For a moment, Sadie thought back to that day. She remembered the audience clapping when she had finished playing. That part had been good.

"I didn't really know anyone at the recital. That made it easier. Now Mom's calling everyone. And all the kids from school will be there," Sadie said.

"Well, if you can't perform in front of

people, you'll have to quit," Henry said matter-of-factly.

Sadie hated the word *quit*. She didn't want to quit . . . but she did want to get out of it.

"I have a question," Henry announced, changing the subject. "I know you said that truffles are some kind of germ you dig up like mushrooms —"

"Not a germ, Henry. A fungus," Sadie corrected.

"Oh, whatever. A fungus, like a mushroom. But I thought truffles were some kind of fancy candy. My mom always makes them around the holidays and gives them to everyone at her office. They're pretty good. I don't think they come out of the ground."

"Well, you're right," said Sadie. "Truffles are also a kind of chocolate. A very sweet and fancy kind of chocolate. And Truffle is a very sweet and fancy kind of puppy. So, I think the name fits either way."

Just then, Truffle ran up and jumped against Henry, knocking him into the mud. The puppy stepped on Henry and walked up his chest, leaving sloppy footprints on his navy jacket. When he got to Henry's face, he gave him a long lick, from his chin to his forehead. Lexi and Sadie stood back and laughed. "I wouldn't say he's fancy," Henry gasped between giggles. "But your puppy is supersweet."

Sadie was laughing so hard she didn't hear her mom call her name at first.

"Sadie, you have a phone call," Mrs. Reynolds said from the deck. "It's a girl named Isa."

Sadie froze. Why would Isa be calling? She looked at Lexi and Henry. "Watch Truffle for me?" she asked before running inside. Her mom gave her a warm smile before passing her the phone.

"Hello?" Sadie said.

"Hi, Sadie. It's Isa." Isa's voice was soft and muffled. "Listen, I just found out that we can't have a piano at the talent show. It's being fixed or some-thing that weekend." She paused. "So, we need you to come up with another act. I hope that's okay — I can count on you, right?" Isa prompted. After a long stretch of silence, Isa asked, "Are you there?"

"Yeah," Sadie mumbled.

"Good. I really appreciate it, Sadie. See you at school tomorrow."

"Yeah," Sadie replied. Then she heard the phone click.

★ Chapter 6 ★

Sadie avoided talking to Isa the next day at school. It seemed like Isa was avoiding her, too.

"What are you going to do?" Lexi asked at lunch.

Sadie stared at her sandwich. "What can I do?" Sadie responded. She didn't feel like she had any options. She would feel bad if she quit the talent show. Isa was trying to do a good thing. Telling people about the wolves was important. But there wasn't anything else that Sadie could do for her

act. Piano was her only real talent, unless you counted her ability to make a banana-and-Nutella sandwich in less than sixty seconds. But no one would want to see that. And it would make for a very short talent show performance.

"Well, the talent show is next weekend, so you've got to come up with something," Lexi said.

Sadie didn't want to think about it. She didn't want to talk about it. She hadn't even told her parents about it! Her mom had asked Sadie what the phone call had been about, but Sadie was too over-whelmed to explain. Isa expected her to come up with a new act? In a week? And perform it in front of an audience?

After school, Sadie wanted some fresh air. She decided to take Truffle back to the dog park. Truffle was so happy, his tail wagged back and forth in the air as they walked.

When they arrived, Sadie saw that someone had set up a giant obstacle course. Truffle saw it, too. His tail wagged even harder.

"You want to give it a try?" Sadie asked.

RRRufff! Truffle pulled against his collar before Sadie could get the leash off. "Calm down, boy. Take it easy. You're still a puppy, you know."

RRRufff! Truffle raced off and started chasing a Shetland sheepdog through a tunnel and over seesaws. Sadie watched in amazement. How had he learned to do all that?

"Hi, Sadie," a voice said.

Sadie turned to see Isa. She was holding her clipboard again.

"I'm collecting more donations," Isa said. "I'm so glad you're here." She tapped the clipboard with her pen twice and stopped.

Thoughts raced through Sadie's brain. Now was the time to tell Isa she couldn't be in the talent show. She would do it nicely, but she had to do it now. Then she noticed Isa looked a little different — a little sad.

Sadie took a deep breath. She wondered if, when she opened her mouth, she would find that she didn't have enough words. Or maybe she'd have way too many.

But Isa spoke before Sadie. "I'm really sorry, Sadie. I had no idea that there wouldn't be a piano for the talent show."

Isa's voice was low. Sadie missed her perky smile.

"Piano is my only talent," Sadie said. "I can't do anything else. I can't juggle or sing, and I definitely can't ride a unicycle. My dad is a really good break-dancer, which is funny, but I can't do that either —"

"Is that Truffle?" Isa interrupted.

Sadie looked up. Truffle was still following the long-haired sheepdog around the course. When the dogs came to the end, the sheepdog's owner reached down and gave them both big pats. Then he held up a hoop and started waving it. The dogs took turns leaping through the hoop. Truffle seemed to sail through the air.

"Wow," Isa said under her breath. "Does he do that for you?"

"I've never tried," Sadie admitted. "I usually just throw a ball or a Frisbee."

"How did he learn to jump like that?" Isa asked.

"I don't know. He just does it," explained Sadie.

The two girls stood in silence. They watched the other owner pet the two dogs before gathering all the obstacle course equipment.

Sadie waved a thank-you as the man left the park. "Truffle!" she called. Her fluffy pup came running, his tongue flapping out the side of his mouth.

Sadie had been so happy watching her puppy that she almost forgot what she needed to do. She needed to get out of the talent show. Sadie bent down to welcome Truffle back. "You know," she started, not looking Isa in the eye. "I really can't be in the talent show. I need a piano. I'm super sorry." When Isa didn't reply right away, Sadie kept talking. "I could help sell tickets or something."

"We really need talent acts," Isa said. "And you'll be perfect. You don't need a piano."

Sadie looked up. She was confused.

The sad look was gone from Isa's face. Her blue eyes were bright and her smile was back. "You can perform," she said,

writing something down on her trusty clipboard. "You and Truffle can do tricks!"

"Oh, no," Sadie insisted. "I don't even know the right commands. And he's way too young." When Sadie looked down, Truffle was staring at her. He barked. He gave her that hopeful expression. Sadie knew he wanted to do his trick, but now was not the time.

"Sadie, you will be so great! Dog tricks at a talent show to help save the wolves. How fabulous is that?" Isa bit the end of her pen and studied her clipboard.

"But we don't have enough time," Sadie said. "It will take tons of practice."

"Don't worry. Look, Truffle is already practicing." Isa pointed at the puppy.

Truffle was spinning around at full speed.

"No, Truffle," Sadie said. "Truffle, no," she repeated. "Not now."

The puppy did not stop. He didn't even slow down. He spun around and around. He went faster and faster. He looked like he was just inches from catching his tail. Sadie saw the silver stars start to whirl into the air. They swirled around her. As she watched them, she seemed to forget all her concerns.

She felt a burst of confidence. What had she been so worried about? This would be great! "We can practice," Sadie heard herself say. "We can do it, for the wolves."

"Really?" Isa asked.

"Really." Sadie had never been so sure of herself. She looked down at Truffle. "Stop," she directed, and the puppy did just that. He sat down and looked up at Sadie, his eyes twinkling.

"I'm so excited," said Isa. She had stopped writing and was just smiling at Sadie. "Thanks. You will be awesome. You will too, Truffle." Isa tousled the puppy's curls and then walked away with a skip in her step.

"Awesome," Sadie repeated. But as Isa walked away, doubt began to creep back in. What had she gotten herself into — again?

⭐ Chapter 7 ⭐

Truffle's trick. It was all Sadie could think about. She had had the perfect chance to get out of the talent show, but then Truffle had worked his magic. When he started spinning — and the stars started swirling — Sadie had changed her mind. She had, all at once, felt like she could take on the world.

Was it Truffle's trick that changed her mind? Did it make her feel like she could be in the talent show? Sadie didn't like that idea. She wanted to make her own

decisions. She was sure there was some-thing unusual about that trick. Sadie needed some answers, so she needed to go to the one place she could ask the right questions.

"Mom, Dad!" she called out as she pulled on her sneakers. "I'm running over to Power's Pets. I'm taking Truffle with me."

Before she was done tying her shoes, both her parents appeared in the front hall.

"Are you going to get more supplies for the show?" her mom asked.

"Don't forget to stock up on treats. You'll need them," her dad added.

Sadie smiled and sighed. Her parents were so excited. Mr. Reynolds knelt down and gave Truffle's belly a big rub. The puppy wiggled around on his back and whimpered happily. Truffle was almost as excited about the talent show as Sadie's parents. They didn't care that Sadie wasn't

playing the piano. If anything, they were even more pleased that Sadie and Truffle were performing together.

"I won't forget," Sadie said. Actually, she didn't think she'd need treats. Truffle usually did all of the obstacles and other tricks without expecting a treat at the end. He did it for fun.

Sadie clipped the leash to her pup's collar and made sure she had the money her dad had given her. "See you soon," she

said with a wave. Her parents waved back and watched her go.

Truffle trotted along beside her. They had practiced all morning, but he did not seem tired at all. He had jumped through her hula hoop close to fifty times. Sadie discovered he could beg. Once, he even jumped on his hind feet. Truffle just liked to show off.

"Practice makes perfect," Sadie mumbled to herself, but she was still worried. She didn't really know how to get Truffle to perform specific tricks. He just did what he felt like.

When she heard the familiar bell on the Power's Pets door, she felt better. Sadie had come to the store for answers, and she was about to get them.

"Well, here are two of my favorites," Mr. Power announced as soon as he saw them.

"Two of my favorites," Mango echoed from his high perch.

"How are you two getting along?" Mr. Power asked, ignoring his feathered friend.

Truffle barked. Sadie didn't know how to answer the question. She decided she should start at the beginning and try to tell Mr. Power everything.

"Truffle is the best puppy. I really love him. He makes me laugh, and he is a great friend. My parents adore him, and my dad doesn't sneeze," she began. "But I can't play piano at the talent show, so now we have to do tricks . . . in front of people. And Truffle seems pretty excited, but I'm pretty nervous. I don't know why I said I'd do it, but I did. I think Truffle's special trick has something to do with it. Something strange." Sadie paused and took a breath.

While Sadie was talking, Mr. Power listened closely, nodding his head and rubbing his whiskers. "Why do you think his

trick has something to do with it?" the old man asked.

"I'm not totally sure," she confessed. "But the first time he did it, we were here. It was the time I told Isa that Truffle was mine. The next time he did his trick, I agreed to play piano in the talent show," she explained. "And the last time, I didn't even ask him to do the trick. He did it all by himself."

"What happened then?" asked Mr. Power.

"That time, I ended up saying we'd do dog tricks for the talent show since there was no piano. We don't know many tricks at all." She bit her upper lip.

"This has become complicated, hasn't it?" Mr. Power murmured.

Sadie nodded. She watched as the owner of the pet center ran his hand over Truffle's back, then up and down his legs. He used a mini flashlight to look in his ears.

He held the puppy's chin and looked in his eyes.

"There's nothing wrong with this puppy," he announced. "He should be able to hear when you ask him to do a trick, and when you don't." He stared into the puppy's shiny eyes again. "Isn't that so, Truffle?"

The puppy's head drooped. He walked over to Sadie and rested his chin on her feet.

Mr. Power turned to the puppy's owner. "Sadie, one thing I can tell you is that

Truffle comes from a long line of perform-ing dogs."

"Do you mean like 'Best in Show' dogs? When dogs compete to be the best dog of their breed?" Sadie asked, feeling a thrill.

"Not exactly," the man replied. "I mean dogs who do tests of agility, like obstacle courses, or dogs that do fun tricks for their owners. Truffle comes from a family of dogs that like lots of attention and applause."

"Oh, Truffle loves attention," Sadie agreed.

"That may be why he's doing his special trick on his own, but I can't be sure," Mr. Power admitted.

"So what should I do?" Sadie asked.

"I think you should believe in yourself. And you should trust Truffle. He's a good dog," the old man said. "The two of you make a great team and you'll be wonder-ful in a talent show."

Just then, the door opened and a customer walked in. "Excuse me," Mr. Power said, and he walked toward the front door.

"Believe in yourself!" Mango repeated. "Great team!"

Sadie and Truffle looked up at the glorious bird. "That's easy for you to say," Sadie mumbled, and she led her puppy out the door.

✦ Chapter 8 ✦

All week, Sadie did what she did best. She practiced. It had worked with the piano recital, and she would make it work for the talent show, too. If she wasn't at school or doing homework, she was in the backyard with Truffle, going over drill after drill.

Truffle loved the attention. He trotted up and down the seesaw like a pro. Sadie held up the hoop higher and higher. Each time, he jumped through with a happy bounce. He playfully lifted his front paws

to beg. These were the only tricks that Sadie knew how to ask Truffle to do, so they practiced them over and over.

Each night, as soon as it was dark, they went inside. There, Sadie recited the introduction to their act. She had written a little speech about wolves and dogs. She knew it by heart.

"Practice makes perfect," she kept reminding herself.

Friday morning, in art class, Isa walked right over to Sadie, Lexi, and Henry's table. "Hey, guys," she said.

"Hi," the three friends answered, but Sadie didn't look up from her clay sculpture. She thought it was starting to look more like a dog, but Jerome Kincaid said it looked like a mastodon.

"I hope I'll see you all at the Save the Wolves talent show tomorrow," Isa said. "Sadie, I can't wait to see Truffle's tricks. My mom printed the programs at

her work, and you are going to be our final act."

"Wow. That's a real honor," declared Lexi.

"Really?" Sadie asked. The other two girls nodded. Sadie did her best to look pleased, but she could only think one thing: Going last gave her more time to get the jitters.

"You'll be great," her dad reassured her at dinner on Friday night.

"How do you know?" Sadie asked.

"Well, I don't," he admitted, "because you wouldn't let us watch you practice. But I have a good feeling."

"It's true, Sadie," her mom said. "You've practiced so much, all by yourself. I feel bad that you've done it all on your own."

"I wasn't on my own," Sadie said. "I had Truffle."

The puppy lifted his head from where

he sat at Sadie's feet. *Rrruff! Rrruff!* Truffle put his front paws on the edge of her dinner chair and wagged his tail.

"That's right, boy. You love to show off, don't you?" Sadie scratched Truffle under the chin. She felt sure the sweet puppy was on her side, but she still didn't quite understand his special trick.

When Sadie woke up, the morning sun was shining in her window. Sadie was still in a daze, and words from her dream kept repeating in her head. It took her a

moment to remember where she had heard them before. The voice was Mango's silly squawk. The bird was saying, "Believe in yourself. Great team!"

Those were the same words he had said when she was at Power's Pets. It had been right after she had talked to Mr. Power about Truffle's trick.

"Great team," she whispered to herself. Her mind twisted and turned around the phrase. She thought about every time she'd felt confident enough to say yes to Isa. "Of course!"

Truffle was still sleepy, too. The puppy waddled over to her bed and blinked at her.

"You weren't trying to make me do something I didn't want to do at all, were you?" she asked her puppy as he jumped onto the bed and nuzzled her face. "You just wanted me to believe in myself. You wanted me to have enough confidence to do what I really wanted."

Sadie thought about it and knew it was true. She now realized she had wanted to help with the talent show. She had been worried about performing, but she had really wanted to help raise money for wolves. Truffle's trick had given her the extra boost of courage to say yes.

"Thank you, boy," Sadie said, ruffling his ears. "Now we just need the confidence to go out there and do our act today!" Sadie swung her legs out of bed. "It'll be easier with your special trick." Truffle cocked his head to one side and gave Sadie

a good, long look. Sadie felt like she should explain her thoughts to her puppy. "You know, if I ever get nervous, you can just do your trick. Then I'll have all the confidence in the world."

Truffle sneezed and wandered away. "Oh, come on," Sadie said. "You're my good luck charm! I know you'll do it, just like you did before."

"Our final act is here!" Isa announced when she saw Sadie and her family walk through the door later that day. "How is our star?" Isa asked, leaning down to give Truffle a pat.

"He's great," Sadie answered. "We both are." Ever since she had realized the power of Truffle's trick, Sadie was no longer worried about performing. She knew she could get Truffle to do his trick whenever she needed a confidence boost, so she wouldn't get flustered.

Sadie's parents went to sit down in the auditorium, while Sadie stayed with Isa. "Since there isn't enough room backstage," Isa explained, "all the acts are just hanging out in the hall. Here's the program, so you know when to go on."

"Thanks, Isa. You've done a great job," Sadie said. Sadie looked around and saw a lot of people in fancy costumes. Carmen and Alexei from fifth grade were dressed up like salsa dancers. There were a lot of kids with musical instruments: an accordion, three violins, a banjo, and a trombone, but no piano. Now, in her head, Sadie was laughing at herself. Why had she ever thought that piano was her only talent?

Sadie and Truffle sat and waited while the other acts performed. She heard laughter and applause. Slowly, as the time passed, she started to feel a little concern seep in. Her chest felt tight. She caught herself biting her lip. She reassured herself by petting

Truffle, who sat calmly at her side, his pink tongue dangling.

Sadie had decided to wait to use Truffle's trick until right before she went on. She wanted the magic to be extra powerful for when they performed. She looked at the program: two acts away. It wouldn't be long now.

⭐ Chapter 9 ⭐

When Sadie heard Isa announce the act before hers, she stood up. "Okay, Truffle, it's time," she said. She clapped and said, "Bet you can't catch it."

Truffle stayed put.

"Didn't you hear me, boy?" Sadie asked. She clapped again and said, "Bet you can't catch it."

Truffle looked her in the eye. He shook his head, his ears flapping back and forth.

From the puppy's expression, she was certain he was refusing to do his special

trick. "No?" Sadie asked. "What do you mean no?" Sadie was shocked. "But I need you to do it now. Please!" she begged.

Truffle stayed still.

Sadie tried to think. Why would he refuse to do the trick at that moment, when she needed it the most?

"Sadie!" Isa called from the stage door. "You're next. We have to organize your props while the other act is performing. Come on!"

"But I can't," Sadie said.

Isa put her clipboard down on the floor and walked over to Sadie.

Sadie raked her bottom teeth across her top lip.

"Sadie," Isa said, "you've been practicing all week. I know you can do this."

"How do you know?"

"I saw you at your piano recital. You were great," Isa explained.

"What?" asked Sadie, surprised.

"My brother has the same piano teacher as you, so I was there to see him. You were really awesome. I can't perform in front of crowds like that. You were so calm. That's why I asked you to be in the talent show."

Sadie stared at Isa. She could hardly believe what the other girl was saying, but Isa's face was kind and sincere. Sadie thought she had been a mess at the piano recital. She had been so nervous!

"Come on," Isa said. "I'll be right backstage. But you won't be out there alone. You have Truffle!"

Sadie nodded and gathered up the props. Isa grabbed her clipboard. Truffle trotted along next to them.

Mr. Haney, the art teacher, had just finished his routine. He had made supersized wolves out of twisty balloons. His face was bright red when he walked by.

"Break a leg!" he said to Sadie between quick, short breaths. Sadie didn't say anything back. She just swallowed.

"And now," Isa said, holding a microphone, "is our last act. Please welcome Sadie Reynolds and Truffle!"

Sadie could hardly feel her hands as she reached for the microphone. She stared at the dark audience. She could only see shadows at first. Then she saw her mom and dad. Her grandma. Aunt Monica. Lexi, Max, and Henry were there, too.

She had found their faces, but she could not find any words.

She looked down at Truffle, who blinked at her with trusting eyes. The auditorium was quiet. Then Sadie thought she heard someone say something. It sounded like it was coming from the back of the room. Sadie squinted and could just make out a figure standing in the doorway. It looked like Mr. Power.

"Believe in yourself!" the voice said. "Great team!"

As Sadie looked closer, she thought she could make out the shape of something perched on the old man's shoulder. That something had a beak, a body, and a long, feathered tail. Mango!

"Great team!" The voice was clearer this time, and so was the message. Sadie glanced at Truffle and he looked her right in the eye. She knew what she had to do.

"Good afternoon," Sadie began slowly,

and then the words just tumbled out. "This is Truffle, my dog. He's very special to me, and he wouldn't be here today if it weren't for wolves." Sadie took a deep breath and reminded herself not to rush. "The wolf is the ancestor of every breed of dog. And just like dogs are an important part of many human families, wolves play an important role in the wild."

Sadie stopped there and took another deep breath. "Wolves are amazing. They live in packs and rely on one another. Over time, dogs have learned to trust humans the same way that wolves trust one another. Now people and dogs share a special bond." She glanced at Truffle and smiled. "We are a pack. We are a team. Thanks for coming out today and helping us help the wolves."

The audience clapped. Sadie had finished her speech, and it was pretty good! She sighed with relief, but she felt like she had forgotten something.

She looked at Truffle. He cocked his head to one side and looked back at her. *RRRufff!*

"Oh, that's right," she exclaimed. "And now for some tricks!"

With that, Truffle bounced up and jumped on his hind feet over and over. Sadie giggled. They hadn't practiced that! She tapped the tunnel, and Truffle raced through. Then he zipped back through it and ran up the seesaw. He stopped in the middle — with both ends of the seesaw in the air — and balanced there. Sadie threw a Frisbee, and he leaped off the seesaw to catch it. The audience cheered. Next, Truffle stood on his hind legs and begged.

"Our final trick is the hoop. Let's see how high Truffle can jump!" Sadie announced. At first, she held it close to the ground. Truffle trotted through.

"Should I go higher?" she asked the audience, and lifted the hoop to her knee.

Truffle leaped through before the audience could answer.

"Should I raise it higher?" The audience clapped. Now Sadie raised it to the middle of her thigh. Truffle gazed at the hoop, took a step back, and then bounded forward. He cleared the hoop with room to spare.

Sadie had thought they would stop there, but Truffle turned around. He was ready to jump again.

"Should we try it one more time?" she asked. The audience cheered. Some of them stood up. Truffle barked with excitement. "Are you sure?" This time, she was asking her puppy. Truffle barked again.

Sadie held the hoop in front of her with one hand. The bottom reached her waist. Truffle had only jumped this high once before. "Ready, boy?" she asked. Truffle barked again. He backed up a couple of steps and started running. As he neared

the hoop, Sadie could see him push off with his strong back legs. He soared into the air. But as he flew toward the hoop, Sadie realized he was aiming right at her! All at once, she let go, held out her hands, and squeezed her eyes shut. The next thing she knew, Truffle was safe in her arms.

The audience stood up and cheered. Truffle licked Sadie's face as she held him

tight. "We definitely didn't practice that," Sadie whispered in her puppy's ear. Sadie looked out at the audience and found the faces of her family and friends. At that moment, she knew all the hard work had been worth it.

In just a few short moments, she and Truffle were surrounded by those same people — the ones who told her all along that she'd be great.

Everyone took a turn congratulating her. Isa joined the happy group, too.

"It was better than piano," her grandma insisted.

"Truffle sure loves to perform," said Henry, scratching the puppy under his chin.

"I knew you could do it," Mr. Power said.

"There was a moment when I wasn't so sure," Sadie admitted. "But when I heard Mango call out, I knew I could do it, too."

Mr. Power looked at her, and so did her parents and her friends. "Mango called out?" Mr. Power said uncertainly. He turned and looked closely at the colorful parrot on his shoulder. "I didn't hear anything."

Lexi, Max, and Henry all shook their heads.

"Yes," Sadie said confidently. "I am sure of it. He said, 'Great team.'"

"Really?" Mr. Power mused. "Funny, I didn't hear him. Maybe it was just in your head?"

Sadie looked at the bird and wondered if that was possible. "Mango?" she asked. For once, the bird did not respond. He lifted one of his feet and pecked it with his beak. Sadie wondered what she had heard. Was the voice really in her own head?

RRRufff! Truffle insisted.

"Yes, Truffle," Mr. Reynolds said, bending down to pet the puppy. Truffle put his front paws on the man's leg. "You did a good job."

"Yes, definitely," Sadie's mom agreed. "But I think Truffle's best trick was helping our Sadie see how talented she is."

Sadie looked around at all the people who had been there for her. It felt pretty amazing. She and Truffle were a team, but there were a lot of other members of their team, too.

Truffle barked again. He stepped into the middle of the circle that they had all made. He spun around twice, and then he bent down and bowed.

They all clapped for Truffle, the little dog with the special tricks. Sadie clapped and cheered the loudest. She could not have been more proud of her puppy, and she was proud of herself, too.

More Puppy Powers!

Puppy Powers

Hide and Go Fetch

KRISTIN EARHART

SCHOLASTIC

PET HOTEL

Look who's checking in at the Pet Hotel!

PET HOTEL
Calling All Pets!

KATE FINCH · SCHOLASTIC

PET HOTEL
A Big Surprise

KATE FINCH · SCHOLASTIC

PET HOTEL
A Nose for Trouble

KATE FINCH · SCHOLASTIC

PET HOTEL
On with the Show!

KATE FINCH · SCHOLASTIC

SCHOLASTIC

WHERE EVERY PUPPY FINDS A HOME

The Rescue Princesses

These are no ordinary princesses—
they're Rescue Princesses!